Drake & Wilde Mysteries
Love in the Time of Pumpkins
Secrets in the Hollow
Shadow of the Horseman

Standalones
A Kiss in the Rain
App-ily Ever After
Once Upon a Winter
The Red Rose
Highland Vow

Short Stories
Seasons of Love: A Short Story Collection
The Eleventh-Hour Pact
A Christmas Yarn
The Farmer and the Belle
Work-Crush Balance

Cedar Creek
Christmas at Cedar Creek
Snowstorm at Cedar Creek
Sunlight on Cedar Creek

Pine Harbor
Allison's Pine Harbor Summer
Evelyn's Pine Harbor Autumn
Lydia's Pine Harbor Christmas

Holiday House

The Christmas Cabin
The Winter Lodge
The Lighthouse
The Christmas Castle
The Beach House
The Christmas Tree Inn
The Holiday Hideaway

Highland Passage

Highland Passage
Knight Errant
Lost Bride

Highland Soldiers

The Enemy
The Betrayal
The Return
The Wanderer

American Hearts

Secret Hearts
Forbidden Hearts
Runaway Hearts

For more information, visit jljarvis.com.

Get monthly book news at news.jljarvis.com.

SHADOW OF THE HORSEMAN

SHADOW OF THE HORSEMAN

DRAKE & WILDE MYSTERY
BOOK 3

J.L. JARVIS

SHADOW OF THE HORSEMAN

Copyright © 2025 by J.L. Jarvis

All rights reserved.

No part of this book may be reproduced in any form or by any electronic or mechanical means, including information storage and retrieval systems, without written permission from the author, except for the use of brief quotations in a book review.

This is a work of fiction. Names, characters, places, and incidents are products of the author's imagination or are used fictitiously. Any resemblance to actual events, locales, or persons, living or dead, is entirely coincidental.

Published by Bookbinder Press

bookbinderpress.com

ISBN (ebook) 978-1-942767-77-0

ISBN (paperback) 978-1-942767-78-7

ONE

"So, there they are. They've just won the war—their independence! And they're thinking, 'Now what?'" Professor Jackson Wilde's voice carried through the lecture hall at Columbia University, his enthusiasm palpable. "The Articles of Confederation, hastily drafted during the war, are proving woefully inadequate. The states are squabbling, the economy is in shambles, and there's a genuine fear that this grand experiment in democracy might fail before it truly begins."

As Jackson clicked to the next slide, a portrait of James Madison appeared on the screen. A male student who always chose the front row leaned toward the pretty young blonde woman beside him. "He kind of looks like Mike Pence," he whispered, his attempt at humor carrying an undercurrent of nervousness.

The blonde shifted slightly away in an almost

imperceptible motion. Her chin rested on her hand while her gaze remained fixed on Professor Wilde with an intensity that made the young man's joke wither in the air between them. A faint flush crept up his neck as he registered her deliberate non-response and resumed typing notes on his laptop.

Jackson raised an eyebrow at the pair. "Enter James Madison, the 'Father of the Constitution.' He and other leaders realize they need a stronger central government, but how do they do that without becoming the very thing they've just fought against?

"Many resisted the idea of a stronger federal government. They feared it would lead to tyranny, the very thing they had just overthrown. This tension between state and federal power would become a defining feature of American politics for generations to come."

As Jackson delved deeper into the Constitutional Convention, a familiar figure slipped quietly into the back of the lecture hall. Arjun, his research assistant, looked unusually agitated. Before Jackson could give thought to why, his phone buzzed in his pocket. With only a few minutes of the class period left, he ignored it and continued his lecture.

"The debates were intense," Jackson said, clicking to a new slide showing the interior of Independence Hall. "Should there be a single executive or a council? How should we apportion representatives? What about the thorny issue of slavery?"

Another buzz came from his phone. Jackson frowned slightly but pressed on. "The compromise that eventually emerged—our current system of a House of Representatives based on population, and a Senate with equal representation for each state—resulted from intense negotiation and, some might even argue, divine inspiration."

Jackson's phone buzzed again. Unable to ignore it anymore, he pulled out his phone and glanced down. Frowning, he read the message from Arjun. *The Seal has been stolen.*

His heart raced, but years of experience helped him maintain his composure. He looked up to see Arjun nodding gravely.

Jackson took a deep breath. His mind raced. "All right, class, I think this is a good place to stop for today. For next time, read chapters seventeen and eighteen in your textbook, focusing on the ratification debates in the various states. Come prepared to discuss how these debates shaped our early national identity."

As the students packed up, Jackson added, "And don't forget, your final papers are due Thursday. My office hours are posted if anyone needs to discuss their topics."

The lecture hall emptied quickly, leaving Jackson alone with Arjun.

"Tell me everything," Jackson said, his voice low as Arjun approached.

Arjun's face was pale, his usual easygoing

demeanor replaced by tense worry. "Iris discovered it this morning." He glanced around to ensure they were alone. "She's been trying to reach you, but your phone must have been on silent."

Jackson took out his phone and saw a series of missed calls and texts from Iris. "How did it happen?" he muttered, more to himself than to Arjun. "With all the security measures we put in place?"

"That's the thing," Arjun said, lowering his voice further. "There were no signs of forced entry. Whoever did this knew exactly what they were doing."

Jackson's mind raced through the possibilities. The number of people who knew about the Seal's location was extremely limited. "Have you told anyone else?" he asked sharply.

Arjun shook his head. "Just you. I came straight here after Iris called."

"Good," Jackson said as he moved toward the door. "Let's keep it that way for now. We need to figure out what happened before we involve anyone else."

Snow was beginning to fall, the first flurries of winter dusting the campus. They rushed outside, their breaths visible in the cold winter air. Jackson's car was parked in a nearby faculty lot. As they walked, Arjun filled him in on the few details they had.

"Iris went to check on the Seal this morning as part of the regular security routine we set up," Arjun explained. "Everything looked normal at first, but when she opened the hidden compartment..."

"It was gone," Jackson finished, his jaw clenched.

Arjun nodded. "She immediately initiated lockdown procedures and started going through the security logs. But so far, nothing's turned up."

They reached the car and brushed off the light dusting of snow before they climbed in. As Jackson started the engine, his phone buzzed again. He glanced at it, his frown deepening.

"Grice," he said grimly. "He wants to meet. Says he has information about the theft."

Arjun's eyes widened. "So, the Cassandra Collective is involved? But if that's so, why would Grice reach out? It doesn't make sense."

Jackson's grip tightened on the steering wheel as he pulled out of the parking lot. "Maybe they're not involved. But if they know about the theft, who else does? And more importantly, who actually has the Seal?"

As they crossed the Henry Hudson Bridge toward Sleepy Hollow, the snow began to fall more heavily, coating the landscape in white. But all Jackson could think of was the Seal. The artifact they had fought so hard to protect was now in unknown hands. Given its power, the consequences could be catastrophic.

"If it's not the Collective, who else could it be?" Arjun mused, breaking the tense silence.

Jackson nodded grimly. "Yeah, good question."

"There were rumors about a group that splintered off from the Wardens," Arjun said.

Jackson nodded. "The Horsemen."

"Horsemen?"

"I know of them, but we'll need to find out more. We know one thing. If they've stolen the Seal, it can't be good."

The Cassandra Collective was dangerous enough, but a group of rogue Wardens with intimate knowledge of the Seal's power? That could be even worse.

"Call Iris," Jackson instructed his car's hands-free system. The phone rang twice before Iris's voice filled the car.

"Iris?"

"Jackson! Thank God. Did Arjun find you?"

"He did," Jackson confirmed. "We're on our way now. Are you okay?"

There was a pause, and when Iris spoke again, her voice was strained. "I'm fine. Just...shaken. I don't understand how this could have happened. We were so careful."

"I know," Jackson said softly. "We'll figure it out. What about the security logs?"

"Nothing there." Iris sighed. "It's like they were ghosts. There were no alarms and nothing unusual on the cameras."

Jackson exchanged a worried glance with Arjun. "All right, we'll be there soon. In the meantime, don't touch anything else. We need to preserve any evidence that's there."

"Of course," Iris agreed. "And Jackson? There's something else. Margaret has been acting strangely." Iris hesitated. "I haven't told you this, but I mentioned to her I was thinking of resigning. I've applied for a few university jobs. But even if those don't pan out, with everything going on, it felt like the right time. Anyway, to be honest, her reaction surprised me. She was understanding to a point, but she seemed preoccupied."

"How so?" Jackson asked.

Iris took a breath. "I mean, I didn't expect her to be devastated, but I thought we had a good professional relationship—that she respected my work. I guess I thought she might be disappointed. But she practically dismissed it after barely a moment of thought and then changed the subject."

"To what?" Jackson looked as confused as Iris felt.

"Well, she did say the Center would miss me, but there were enough volunteers to cover my tours. Then she launched into some, well, pointed questions about our security protocols for the Seal."

Jackson's grip on the steering wheel tightened. "When was this?"

"Yesterday."

"What questions?" Jackson asked, his voice tense. Margaret Verplanck, the head of the Heritage Center, had witnessed the Seal's power firsthand during a hostage situation. While they hadn't shared all the Seal's details with her, she knew enough to be a suspect —a dangerous one.

"She said she was updating the Center's security protocol manual—our vault security, access logs, that sort of thing. It seemed odd at the time because she was more of a curator and manager. An outside company handles our security. Anyway, it could be nothing, but after what happened..." Iris said.

Jackson nodded grimly. "Keep a close eye on her until we get there."

As they ended the call, Jackson's phone buzzed again with another message from Grice. *Time is running out. Meet me at the old lighthouse. Come alone.*

"You can't seriously be considering meeting him," Arjun protested.

Jackson's expression was grim. "At this point, we don't have much choice. If Grice knows something about the Seal, we need that information. If it means walking into a trap, I'm willing to risk it."

The snow was falling heavily now, reducing visibility on the road. Jackson slowed the car and peered through the windshield at the white-shrouded landscape. The familiar sights of Sleepy Hollow seemed somehow different, as if the theft of the Seal had cast a shadow over everything. The Old Dutch Church loomed in the distance, a silent reminder of all that had happened—and might be still to come.

As they approached the town, Jackson made a decision. "Arjun, I'm going to drop you off at the Heritage Center. Help Iris go through the security logs again. Look for anything out of the ordinary, no matter how small. I'll meet Grice."

"Alone? That's not a good idea," Arjun argued. "What if it's an ambush?"

"That's exactly why I need you with Iris," Jackson countered. "If something goes wrong, you two need to be ready to act. And if this meeting with Grice is legitimate, we might get the lead we need."

Arjun didn't look convinced, but he nodded reluctantly. "Just...be careful, okay? We don't know who we can trust, but he's not even on the shortlist."

Jackson's jaw tightened as he pulled up to the Heritage Center. "I know. That's what worries me."

As Arjun got out of the car, Jackson caught his arm. "One more thing. See if you can discreetly look into Margaret's recent activities. Phone records, emails, anything. If she's involved in this somehow..."

Arjun nodded, understanding the implication. "I'm on it."

As Arjun disappeared into the building, Jackson turned the car around and headed toward the old lighthouse. The snow flurries thickened, obscuring the road ahead.

While Jackson navigated the winding roads now blanketed with snow, his thoughts lingered on Grice's possible role in the theft. The Wardens of Liberty had safeguarded the Seal for generations. Its disappearance now wasn't just a breach of security—it was a ticking time bomb. In the wrong hands, the Seal could destroy the principles underpinning American democracy— and God knew what else.

And Grice was somehow involved—Grice, a man who had once been their enemy. The weight of responsibility pressed down on Jackson. The Seal was out there—its power poised to be unleashed. And they were the only ones who could stop it.

Through the snowy haze, the lighthouse beam came into view. Jackson steeled himself. The answers they needed were out there, hidden in the shadows of history and the machinations of secret societies. It was up to him to uncover the truth, no matter the cost.

TWO

The old lighthouse loomed before Jackson, its weathered facade barely discernible through the swirling snow. He parked his car at the base of the structure, the engine's rumble fading into the howling wind. For a moment, he sat still with his hand on the door handle, weighing his options one last time.

Meeting Grice here alone was risky, but the promise of answers—of something that could finally piece it all together—was too tempting to turn back. With a deep breath, Jackson stepped into the biting cold. Snow crunched beneath his feet as he made his way to the lighthouse entrance.

The door creaked open before he could knock and revealed Grice's silhouette against the dim interior light. "Professor Wilde," Grice said, his voice as cold as the air outside. "I was starting to think you wouldn't come."

Jackson stepped inside and shook off the snow. The interior of the lighthouse was chilly, but at least it provided shelter from the howling wind. "Well, I'm here. You said you had information about the Seal."

Grice nodded and gestured for Jackson to follow him up the winding staircase. "It's not just about the Seal anymore. There's a new player, and they're more dangerous than you can imagine."

As they climbed, Jackson's mind raced. The worn stone steps felt treacherous underfoot, and he couldn't shake the feeling that he was walking into a trap. "The Horsemen?" He carefully watched Grice's reaction.

Grice paused on the stairs for a moment but quickly regained his composure and proceeded. "So, you've heard of them. Yes, the Horsemen. A splinter group from the Wardens with a very different agenda."

They reached the top of the lighthouse, where a small room offered a panoramic view of the snow-covered landscape. Wind battered the structure and rattled the windows in their frames. Grice approached a table and spread out a map.

"The Cassandra Collective has been monitoring their movements," Grice explained as he traced a path across the map that connected seemingly random points. "They're gathering resources and recruiting members from both the Wardens and other organizations. And now, they've got the Seal."

Jackson leaned in and studied the map. The locations covered several states. If there was a pattern, he couldn't quite make it out. "How long have you been aware of them?"

Grice's expression grew tense. "We've had suspicions for months, but nothing solid until recently. They're skilled at covering their tracks."

Jackson clenched his fists at his sides. "And why should I believe you? For all I know, the Collective could be behind the theft."

Grice's bitter laugh echoed through the cramped room. "Believe me, Wilde, if we had the Seal, I wouldn't be here talking to you. The Horsemen pose a threat to everyone—the Wardens, the Collective, and your precious democracy."

"What do they want?" Jackson asked, his eyes still fixed on the map.

"Power, of course. But not just any power." Grice lowered his voice as if he feared being overheard. "They believe the Seal is the key to unlocking something far more significant."

"Such as...?"

Grice fixed his grim eyes on Jackson. "The power to reshape reality itself."

Jackson's blood ran cold. "That's impossible. The Seal is powerful, but it can't—"

"Can't it?" Grice interrupted, his eyes glinting in the dim light. "You've seen what it can do. But that's just the surface. The Horsemen have uncovered documents that reveal the Seal's true potential. And they intend to use it."

Outside, the wind howled with renewed fury. Jackson paced the small room, overwhelmed by this new information. The wooden floorboards creaked beneath his feet, a counterpoint to the storm's rage. "What documents?"

"Copies of Warden texts, " Grice said with a knowing look.

"But how? The Wardens have guarded the Seal's secrets for generations."

Grice's expression grew grim. "That's the unsettling part. We suspect they have a mole, someone high up in the Warden hierarchy—someone with access to the most closely guarded secrets."

The revelation was daunting. The situation was even more serious than Jackson had imagined. "Who could it be?"

Grice shook his head. "We don't know, but we're working on it. That's why I reached out to you. Your connections and insight into the Wardens could be crucial."

Jackson stopped pacing and fixed a hard stare on Grice. "Why are you telling me this? What's in it for the Collective?"

Grice's expression hardened as a flash of something—perhaps fear—crossed his face. "Self-preservation. The Horsemen won't stop at merely reshaping America. They'll target everyone who knows about the Seal. Our knowledge poses a threat. So, they'll come for me, for you—and for your lovely Dr. Drake."

Jackson tamped down his instinctive reaction. "So, you want to work together?" He swallowed the bitter taste in his mouth. The thought of joining forces with

Grice and the Collective, after everything they had done, felt like betraying everything he stood for.

"A temporary alliance," Grice corrected, his tone businesslike. "To stop the Horsemen and retrieve the Seal. After that...well, we can resume our usual animosity."

Jackson considered his options. Trusting Grice was risky, but if his claims about the Horsemen were accurate, they needed all the assistance they could find. The fate of the nation—and perhaps the world—was at stake.

"I need to talk about this with my team," Jackson said at last, his voice strained with the gravity of the decision.

"Your team," Grice said with a hint of condescension, "had better not take too long." He reached into his coat and pulled out a small, leather-bound book. Its cover was worn, and the pages were yellowed with age. "Take this. It contains some of what we've uncovered about the Horsemen and their plans. But be careful. Knowledge isn't just power. It draws attention."

As Jackson took the book, he could sense the weight of history in his hands. How many secrets were hidden within these pages? And at what price had they been acquired?

Just then, his phone buzzed with a message from Iris. *Emergency at the Center. Come quickly.*

"Trouble?" Grice asked with sharp eyes on Jackson.

"I need to go," Jackson said as he headed toward the stairs. "I'll be in touch about your...offer."

"Don't wait too long, Wilde. The Horsemen won't," Grice called after him, his voice tinged with urgency.

Jackson rushed down the stairs, his thoughts racing faster than his feet. It was nearly too much to fathom—the Horsemen, a mole within the Wardens, and the Seal's true power on the brink of being unleashed.

As he burst out of the lighthouse and into the storm, the wind nearly knocked him off his feet. Snow whipped against his face, sharp and relentless, as he trudged toward the car. Each step felt like a struggle against the storm's might. He clutched his coat tighter. The weight of the leather-bound book pressed against his side—its presence impossible to ignore.

By the time the Heritage Center's familiar glow came into view, the sky had turned a deep, bruised gray. Jackson parked quickly, his tires skidding on the slick pavement. He shoved the door open and hurried inside, pausing only to brush the snow from his coat and stomp his boots.

The warmth of the building did little to ease the tension that waited inside. Iris and Arjun stood in the main office, their expressions heavy with worry. The space, usually so calm and welcoming, felt stifling now.

"What's going on?" Jackson asked, his pulse already racing. He glanced between the two, searching their faces for any hint of what had changed.

Iris looked up, wide-eyed, and spoke in a trembling voice. "It's Margaret. She's gone."

The word hit like a stone in Jackson's chest. "What do you mean *gone*?"

Arjun stepped forward with his laptop open. The blue screen cast a cold light across his face, highlighting the worry etched into his features. "She left about an hour ago, heading home early because of the storm. I got suspicious and checked the security cameras, though." He turned the screen toward Jackson, displaying footage of Margaret hurriedly leaving the building, nervously glancing over her shoulder.

Jackson leaned closer, his eyes glued to the screen. Margaret's movements were jittery, her eyes darting as if she were being followed. Her hurried steps and anxious glances made it clear—she wasn't herself. She looked like someone burdened by a secret too heavy to carry.

"That's not all," Iris said, her voice strained. She held up a small, ornate key, its intricate patterns glinting under the light. "I found this near her desk. It matches the lock on the Seal's container."

Jackson felt a cold weight settle in his chest. Margaret had been there when the Seal's power had been uncovered. She'd seen its significance and understood the danger, so she had to know the sort of risk she was taking.

But the pieces clicked together, each one darker than the last—her odd behavior, her probing questions, and now, her disappearance along with the Seal. It all led to one chilling conclusion.

"She's working with them," Jackson said. The realization hit him like a punch to the gut. "Margaret's with the Horsemen."

Iris gasped while Arjun muttered a curse under his breath.

"Are you sure?" Iris asked, her voice barely above a whisper. "Margaret's been with the Heritage Center for years. She's dedicated her life to preserving history, not...not this."

Jackson ran a hand through his hair. "Think about it: her recent behavior, the questions about security, and now this key. It all fits. And if Grice is right about the Horsemen having a mole in the Wardens..."

"Wait, a mole?" Arjun interrupted with his brow furrowed.

While Jackson quickly filled them in on his meeting with Grice, he watched their expressions shift from surprise to concern to grim determination.

"We need to find her," Jackson said. "If she's involved in the theft, she might lead us to the Seal."

As they gathered coats and equipment to leave, Jackson's phone buzzed again. This time, it was a message from Grice. *I hope you're convinced now. It's time to work together.*

Jackson showed the message to Iris and Arjun.

"Can we trust him?" Iris asked, her voice laced with doubt. "After everything the Collective has done?"

"I don't think we have a choice," Jackson replied grimly. "The Horsemen have the Seal, and now they have Margaret. We're going to need all the help we can get."

Arjun nodded, his expression serious. "I'll start tracking Margaret's phone to see if I can ping her location. And I'll dig deeper into her recent communications to see if there's anything we missed."

"Good," Jackson said. "Let's head to Margaret's office. Maybe we can find something there that'll give us a clue about where she's gone and what she's planning."

As they stepped out of the main area, the usually bustling Center became eerily quiet. As their footsteps echoed in the empty corridors, Jackson's mind whirled with possibilities and fears. The Seal was gone, Margaret was compromised, and an ancient power beyond their understanding was at stake. And somewhere out there, the Horsemen were moving forward with their plans, whatever those plans might be.

They reached Margaret's office door, and Jackson hesitated for a moment before turning the handle.

"All right," he said in a determined hush. "Let's see what secrets Margaret's been keeping."

THREE

The storm raged outside, but within Margaret's office at the Heritage Center, another type of tempest was brewing. Jackson and Iris moved methodically through the room, searching for any clue that could lead them to Margaret or the stolen Seal. The office, once a welcoming space of quiet scholarship, now felt alien and menacing. Every shadow seemed to conceal a secret, and every innocent object was a potential clue.

Jackson brushed his fingers along the spines of the books on Margaret's shelves, pondering how many of them concealed hidden meanings or coded messages. Betrayal hung heavy in the air, making even the familiar surroundings feel sinister.

"I still can't believe it," Iris murmured as she rifled through a stack of papers on the desk. Her hands trembled as she sorted through the documents, each a potential link to Margaret's deception. "Margaret's been a mentor to me since I started here. How could she be involved in something like this?"

Jackson paused his examination of a bookshelf and turned to face Iris. The pain in her voice was palpable, and he felt a surge of protectiveness. Her usually bright eyes were clouded with confusion and hurt. "People aren't always what they seem," he said gently, choosing his words carefully. "Sometimes, the ones closest to us are the ones who can hurt us the most."

Iris met his gaze, her eyes shimmering with unshed tears. The vulnerability in her expression made Jackson's heart ache.

"I know. It's just...hard to accept. I trusted her, Jackson. We all did."

Jackson stepped closer and placed a comforting hand on her shoulder. He sensed the tension in her muscles, weighed down by the burden of betrayal. "We'll figure this out. Margaret's actions don't erase all the good she's done or the positive impact she's had on your life. But right now, we need to find her and the Seal."

For a moment, they stood in silence, the weight of their shared burden heavy between them. The ticking of the antique clock on Margaret's desk felt unnaturally loud, a reminder that time was not on their side. Then, with a deep breath, Iris nodded and returned to her search, her movements more determined than ever.

As Jackson turned back to the bookshelf, something caught his eye. A small, leather-bound volume that resembled the one Grice had given him was wedged between two larger books. It looked innocuous enough, but years of research had taught Jackson to trust his instincts. His heart raced as he pulled it out and flipped it open.

"Iris," he called. His voice was tight with excitement and apprehension. "Look at this."

She rushed over and peered at the pages he held open. The book was filled with handwritten notes, diagrams, and what appeared to be coded messages. The ink varied in color and intensity, indicating entries made over a long period. "Is that...Margaret's handwriting?"

Jackson nodded grimly. He recognized the distinctive slant of Margaret's handwriting. "It is. And look at this symbol." He pointed to a small emblem sketched in the corner of one page—a stylized horseshoe with curves that formed an almost sinister shape.

Iris gasped. "The Horsemen. It can't be..."

"But this proves it. Margaret's with them. Who knows for how long?" The realization took a moment to settle in. Everything they thought they knew about their colleague and friend was a lie.

As they examined the book's contents, a picture began to take shape. Margaret had been collecting information on the Seal and its history, piecing together fragments of lore and legend. More importantly, she'd been gathering data on the Wardens themselves—their structure, methods, and weaknesses. Each page revealed more of Margaret's double life and the extent of her deception.

Jackson reeled from the implications of their discovery. "She was their mole in the Wardens."

Iris's face went pale. "But how? Margaret isn't a Warden. She's always been so committed to the Heritage Center—to preserving history. How could she be involved in a group trying to manipulate it?"

"No, she's not a Warden," Jackson concurred as his mind raced to connect the dots. "But she had access to many of their records through the Heritage Center. More importantly, she had our trust."

Iris shook her head slowly. "This doesn't prove anything except that she was interested in the Wardens. And why wouldn't she be?"

"Think about it, Iris. How many times have we talked about Warden business in front of Margaret, believing she was just a curious historian? And now the Seal is gone, and Margaret along with it."

The realization of how much they had unknowingly revealed struck Iris deeply. She sank into Margaret's chair. "We've been so blind," she whispered, her voice tinged with self-recrimination.

Before Jackson could respond, the door burst open and startled them both. Arjun rushed in with his glasses slightly askew, clutching his laptop tightly to his chest. His usual easygoing demeanor was replaced by an urgency that instantly put Jackson on high alert.

"Guys, you need to see this," Arjun said, slightly out of breath. "I've found something big."

They gathered around as Arjun set down his computer on Margaret's desk. The blue glow of the screen cast an eerie light in the room. "I've been looking into Margaret's recent communications," he explained as his fingers flew over the keyboard. "Some of it was encrypted, and I mean seriously encrypted—military-grade stuff. But I managed to crack some of it. Check out this email thread."

On the screen, a series of messages appeared, each more damning than the last. Margaret had been corresponding with someone using the codename "Rider," discussing plans for the Seal's theft and its transportation to a secure location. The clinical, almost cold tone of the emails sent a shiver down Jackson's spine. This was the Margaret they knew, but a version of her they had never seen before—calculating, secretive, and completely determined to fulfill the Horsemen's mission.

Arjun pointed to the time stamp. "The last message was sent just before she left. *'Package secured. Proceeding to rendezvous point Alpha.'* They've got to be talking about the Seal."

Jackson tried to piece together the puzzle. "Can you trace the recipient's location? If we can find out where this rendezvous point Alpha is, we might be able to intercept them."

Arjun shook his head, frustration clear in his voice. "Not exactly. Whoever 'Rider' is, they're good. Really good. But I managed to narrow it down to a general area." He pulled up a map that highlighted a region just outside of Sleepy Hollow. The area was mostly green, indicating dense forest. "It's mostly wilderness, but there's an old hunting lodge out there that's been abandoned for years. It doesn't show up on most modern maps, but I found references to it in some old land records."

"That has to be it," Iris said, her voice tight with determination. She stood up, her earlier despair replaced by a fierce resolve. "We need to go there. Now. If we hurry, we might catch Margaret before she hands over the Seal."

Jackson nodded as he reached for his coat. "Arjun, contact Grice. Tell him what we've found and where we're going. If he's serious about working together, we might need backup."

As they prepared to leave, gathering what evidence they could, Jackson's phone buzzed with an incoming call. The number was unfamiliar, a string of random digits. Feeling a sense of foreboding, he answered and put it on speaker so Iris and Arjun could hear.

"Hello, Professor Wilde." The voice on the other end wasn't familiar, but there was no mistaking the hint of amusement that sent an icy chill through Jackson.

Jackson's grip on the phone tightened. "Who is this?" he demanded, struggling to keep his voice steady.

A chuckle came through the line. "Oh, I think you know. But if you need a hint, ask your father."

The words struck Jackson like a physical blow, causing him to stagger slightly. Iris reached out to steady him, her touch grounding him in the moment.

"My father? What does he have to do with this?" Jackson barely whispered.

"Everything." The caller's voice took on a more serious tone, the amusement replaced by something darker. "You'll find what you're looking for at the cabin."

"What?" Before he could ask more, the line went dead. He and Iris stared at each other in stunned silence. The only sound in the room was the gentle hum of Arjun's laptop and their own ragged breathing.

Iris placed a hand on his arm. "Jackson?" Though her touch was gentle, her eyes were filled with confusion. "What did he mean about your father?"

He shook his head, his mind reeling from the implications of the call. "I don't know. My father's been out of the picture for years. I assumed that he was dead by now." The admission took its toll on him, bringing up memories and emotions he'd long since buried.

Arjun cleared his throat, shattering the tense silence. "Um, guys? I hate to bring more bad news, but I just got a ping from Margaret's phone. It's moving quickly, heading away from Sleepy Hollow."

Jackson's jaw clenched as he pushed aside his personal turmoil. He would deal with the mystery of his father later. Right now, they had a job to do. "We need to move now. Whatever's going on with my father will have to wait. The Seal is our priority."

As they rushed out of the Heritage Center and into the storm, Jackson's mind reeled with the unsettling feeling that they were stepping into something much larger than they'd imagined. The Horsemen, Margaret's betrayal, and now this mysterious connection to his estranged father? It all felt impossibly tangled like, a web of secrets and lies that threatened to ensnare them.

They piled into Jackson's car, and the engine roared to life as they set off into the snowy night. The windshield wipers struggled against the onslaught of snow, barely maintaining visibility. The streets of Sleepy Hollow were deserted. The storm had driven everyone indoors, leaving Jackson feeling as if they were the only people left in the world, headed toward an uncertain and dangerous future.

"Arjun," Jackson called over his shoulder, his eyes fixed on the perilous road ahead. "Keep tracking Margaret's phone. Let me know if there's any change in direction or if it stops moving."

"On it," Arjun replied with his face lit by the glow of his laptop screen. "Iris, could you help me review Margaret's notes? There might be something in there that could give us an edge."

Iris nodded and pulled out the leather-bound book they'd found in Margaret's office. As she flipped through the pages, her expression grew troubled. "Jackson, some of these notes...they're about you. Your research, your movements. Margaret's been tracking you for months."

The revelation was chilling, yet he forced himself to concentrate on driving. The road narrowed and wound through the forest like a ribbon against the white landscape. Trees loomed on either side, their branches heavy with snow, creating a tunnel-like effect that heightened the sense of isolation.

Suddenly, Arjun's voice cut through the tense silence, "The signal's stopped moving. It's... Wait, that can't be right."

"What is it?" Iris asked, twisting in her seat to look at him.

Arjun's face was a mask of stunned confusion. "According to this, Margaret's phone is at your family's cabin, Jackson. The one in the Adirondacks."

Jackson gripped the steering wheel. "That's impossible. How would Margaret even know about that place?" But even as he said it, a sinking feeling settled in his stomach as he recalled the mysterious phone call. If his father was somehow involved with the Horsemen, then the cabin—a place Jackson had thought was a safe haven—could be compromised.

"Change of plans," Jackson said, his voice tight with determination and a hint of fear. "We're heading to the cabin. Whatever's waiting for us there, we need to face it head-on."

As they changed course, the storm seemed to intensify as if nature itself were trying to impede their progress. The wind howled and buffeted the car from side to side. Snow swirled in mesmerizing patterns before the headlights with an almost hypnotic effect. But Jackson pressed on, driven by a determination born of both duty and a growing personal stake in this mystery.

The drive stretched on for hours before the familiar shape of the cabin loomed ahead. It was a dark silhouette against the snowy backdrop, both inviting and threatening on the stormy night. As they got closer, Jackson sensed they could be walking into a trap. But the Seal was at stake, and the mystery of his father's involvement loomed over him. He had no choice but to move ahead.

"Be ready for anything," he cautioned as they pulled up to the cabin.

The storm had died down to a gentle snowfall, but the sudden stillness heightened the tension. The oppressive silence was broken only by the gentle tapping of snow against the car's cooling engine.

They approached the cabin cautiously. The crunch of snow beneath their feet sounded unnaturally loud in the stillness. Jackson reached for the door but hesitated before turning the knob. The familiar feel of the worn brass in his hand flooded him with childhood memories, now tinged with suspicion and fear.

The door swung open with a creak to reveal a sight none of them had expected. The cabin's interior was warm and well-lit, with a fire crackling in the hearth. An older man, his silver hair neatly combed, sat calmly at the old oak table, his posture straight and dignified. As they entered, he looked up, and a small smile played at the corners of his mouth.

"Hello, Son," he said, his voice rich and familiar despite the years of absence. "It's been a long time."

Jackson stood frozen in the doorway while his mind

raced to make sense of what he was seeing. The man in front of him felt both familiar and strange, like a ghost from his past. "Dad?"

Years of unanswered questions hung in the air.

Jackson's father stood with deliberate and controlled movements. Although he was dressed casually, he exuded an undeniable air of authority. "I imagine you have questions," he said, his tone maddeningly calm considering the circumstances. "Why don't you all come in? We have a lot to discuss."

FOUR

The cabin felt suffocating despite the vaulted, beamed ceiling. Jackson stood rigid, his gaze fixed on his father. He was older now but with the same imposing presence Jackson remembered from childhood.

Nathan Wilde gestured toward the worn leather chairs near the fireplace. "Please, sit," he said, his voice heavy with unspoken history. "We need to talk."

Jackson stayed where he was, glaring at his father with narrowed eyes. Twenty years of silence had led to this moment, and now the pain of abandonment and everything his father had inflicted on him came rushing back.

The crackling fire cast dancing shadows across the room. "You expect me to sit?" Jackson replied, making no move. His body was tense, ready either to flee or to fight at a moment's notice, but his father was perfectly calm as if he'd expected him. And then the realization came to him—he did. "You lured me here. That phone call..."

"It was Crane. I knew you'd recognize my voice."

"Yeah, and you knew I wouldn't come here if I thought it was you." Jackson didn't care how biting his tone was. No matter how bitter he felt, his father deserved it.

Nathan looked down and nodded. "I thought you might be angry."

Jackson smirked and nodded.

"Everything I've done has been to protect you," Nathan said.

"Like missing Mom's funeral?" Jackson's voice was razor-sharp. "Or was that just part of your 'undercover operation,' too?"

Nathan flinched as a shadow of pain crossed his face. "That was unavoidable. And gut-wrenching."

Something in his father's uncharacteristic display of emotion caught Jackson off guard. They were both teetering on the edge of feelings neither wanted to share with the others present, so Jackson reluctantly sat down. He pushed aside thoughts of his personal life, a coping mechanism he had mastered since childhood.

"Where is Margaret?" he demanded, skipping the small talk.

Nathan's expression hardened. "She was here, but she's gone now. You've stepped into something much bigger than you can imagine."

"Oh, we can imagine plenty," Iris replied, her voice sharp with controlled anger. "Margaret betrayed us.

She stole the Seal. And you," she said, pointing at Nathan, "are involved."

Nathan nodded slowly as if weighing his next words. "You're right, but there's much more to the story." He turned his gaze to Jackson. "Son, do you remember the stories I told you as a child about our family history?"

Jackson's brow furrowed as childhood memories flickered through his mind. "You mean the stories about secret keepers and guardians of some great mystery?" His tone was laced with skepticism. "Those were just bedtime stories."

"They weren't just stories." Nathan leaned forward. "Our family has been protecting something for generations. Something powerful."

Compelled by the tension, Jackson stood up again. He began to pace the room as the weight of his father's words sank in. "So, this is about the Wardens? The Horsemen?"

Nathan nodded grimly. "Yes, the Horsemen believe the Seal should be used to reshape society, but they don't understand the true danger it poses."

"And where do you stand in all of this?" Jackson stopped pacing. His voice was dangerously low. "Are you a Warden, or are you with the Horsemen?"

His father's expression softened slightly, revealing the pain etched in the lines of his face. "I'm your father. Everything I've done is for you and our family's legacy."

"That's not an answer," Jackson snapped.

"No, it's not," his father agreed as he stood to

confront his son. "But the situation isn't that simple. I've been working undercover, infiltrating the Horsemen to understand their plans and try to stop them from within."

Iris stood up now and stepped closer. "What about Margaret? Is she part of your little undercover operation?"

Nathan's face darkened. "She was...a complication. I thought I could use her position at the Heritage Center to gather intel, but she went rogue."

Jackson ran his hand through his hair, frustration evident in every motion. "She stole the Seal. Now she's with the Horsemen, and they have the Seal's power."

Nathan nodded. "Yes. And if they unlock its full power..." He leaned forward, his gaze steady. "The Seal wasn't just a symbol of authority—it was a tool, and one the Founding Fathers feared more than they revered it. Its power lies in its ability to disrupt systems—weapons, communication networks, even human biology. During the Revolutionary War, they saw its effects firsthand when it melted British muskets mid-battle. But overuse proved dangerous—it nearly killed one of their own after prolonged exposure. That's why they decided it must never be wielded by one man or one group. It had to be hidden, protected."

Jackson frowned. "So, what is it?"

Nathan shook his head. "I don't know. It's something we haven't been able to identify. All we know is it destabilizes anything it interacts with—machines, structures, even minds. That's why the Horsemen must be stopped."

Arjun, who had been quietly listening, stepped forward and pulled out his laptop. "Where's the base? The Horsemen's main operations?"

Nathan shook his head. "It's not that simple. Their base is heavily guarded, both physically and digitally. You'll need more than your equipment. Getting in will require inside knowledge and careful planning."

Jackson leaned back in his chair as the weight of the information crashed down on him. "Why now, Dad? Why reveal all this after years of silence?"

"After your mother died, I faced a choice—stay and risk having the Horsemen find you or disappear and take the fight to them. I chose the latter." Nathan's voice was quiet but heavy.

Jackson's fists clenched. "And you didn't think I deserved to know?"

"You were a child," Nathan replied, his voice rising. "Do you have any idea how many families of Wardens the Horsemen have destroyed? They kill anyone who stands in their way. If they had known I was alive, they would have come for you, too."

"And now?" Jackson's tone was biting.

Nathan looked at him, a mix of regret and determination in his eyes. "Now they've grown bold enough to move openly. The time for hiding is over. The Horsemen are closer than ever to their goal, and we need every ally we can gather to stop them."

"You said 'we.' Who exactly are you working with?"

Iris, who had been watching the exchange intently, spoke up.

A small smile played at the corners of Nathan's mouth as he glanced toward the window. "Ah, that's where things get interesting. You've already met one of my associates, though I doubt it was a pleasant encounter."

Jackson was about to respond when the cabin door creaked open, and a cold gust of wind blew in as a figure stepped inside.

"I hope I'm not interrupting," Grice said from the doorway, his tone sharp.

Jackson's instincts kicked in, and he positioned himself between Grice and the others. "What the hell are you doing here?"

Grice ignored Jackson's glare and casually brushed the snow off his coat. "We're here for the same reason. The Horsemen's plan needs to be stopped." He dropped a dossier onto the table and sent Jackson's notes fluttering to the floor. "You don't have to trust me," he snapped, his usual smugness replaced by intensity. "But here's why you should listen."

He flipped the folder open, revealing grainy photos of Horsemen operatives and intercepted communications. "These are their key players. Their plans. I've been feeding false intel to the Horsemen for months to buy us time."

"And why should we believe you?" Iris asked with her arms crossed.

Grice pulled a worn photo from the file, his hand

trembling slightly. It was a family portrait, the edges yellowed with age. "Because they killed my wife and daughter," he said quietly. "I've been playing both sides to ensure they don't succeed. I don't care if you hate me, but if we don't stop them, no one else will."

Jackson looked between his father and Grice with his mind reeling. Everything he thought he knew about the past few years—his family history and the nature of their conflict—was being turned upside down.

"He's right," Nathan said.

Jackson stared at his father, unsure of what to believe anymore. Finally, with a voice that sounded steady despite the turmoil inside, he said, "Tell us what's going on—everything from the beginning. No more half-truths or omissions."

His father gestured for everyone to gather closer. "It all started generations ago, with the creation of the Seal. But to understand its true power and the danger we now face, we need to go back even further—to the very foundations of this nation."

As Nathan Wilde began speaking, the cabin seemed to fade away, replaced by a vast span of history and a looming threat that hung in the balance. It all hinged on the Seal and a family legacy Jackson was only beginning to understand.

※

As THE HOURS PASSED, the group moved to the cabin's small kitchen. Iris was busy making coffee, while

Arjun sat at the table, furiously typing notes on his laptop. Grice paced by the window, occasionally peering out into the snowy darkness. Jackson and his father stood apart from the others, their voices low but intense.

"You could have reached out," Jackson said, the hurt evident in his voice despite his attempt to mask it. "All these years, I thought you must be dead."

His father's face creased with regret. "I wanted to, Son. But the deeper I got into the Horsemen's organization, the more dangerous it became. I couldn't risk them using you against me."

Jackson shook his head, struggling to reconcile the man before him with the father he remembered. "And Mom? Did she know?"

A shadow passed over the elder Wilde's face. "Your mother... That's a complicated story, Jackson. One we don't have time for right now."

Before Jackson could press further, Grice cleared his throat. "As touching as this reunion is, we have pressing matters to discuss."

Iris returned with a tray of steaming mugs, passing them out before taking a seat next to Arjun. "Grice is right," she said, her voice steady despite the tension in the room. "We need to know what we're up against. What exactly are the Horsemen planning to do with the Seal?"

Nathan sighed heavily and joined them at the table. "The Seal isn't merely a symbol or a key to hidden knowledge. It's...something else entirely. Something the

Founding Fathers believed was too dangerous to be wielded by any one person or group."

Arjun stopped typing, his fingers poised over his keyboard. "Well, obviously. I mean, melting firearms was a pretty good sampling of what it can do. But what exactly are we dealing with here?"

"Power," Grice answered, his usual smug tone replaced by one of genuine concern. "The kind that defies explanation."

Arjun pushed back from his computer. "There's always an explanation."

Iris looked up from her notes, carefully dating and attributing each piece of information. Old habits from her academic days had taught her the hard way that unprotected research could be stolen by those you trust the most.

"Of course, there's an explanation. We just don't know what it is," Jackson said wryly.

"Magic?" Iris said with a flippant shrug.

Arjun gave her a tolerant smile. "I don't believe in magic—just really good tech. But in this case, it can't be some sort of advanced technology if the forefathers had access to it."

Nathan nodded grimly. "Whatever it is, the Horsemen see themselves as the true heirs to the Founders' vision. They're convinced they know better than the American people what's best for the nation. So, they plan to use the Seal to fundamentally reshape American society."

A heavy silence fell over the room as the implications sank in. Jackson struggled to process the enormity of the threat they faced.

"But how?" Iris practically whispered. "How can an object have that kind of power?"

"There are theories," Nathan said, his voice low. "But no one knows for sure. What we do know is that the Seal can change everything—its power goes beyond our understanding."

"Some say it's of extraterrestrial origin, a tool given to the Founders by beings beyond our understanding. Given the emerging evidence of UAPs—unidentified aerial phenomena—it's not unthinkable," Grice said.

Arjun's brow furrowed. "You're not suggesting the Founding Fathers were abducted by aliens."

"No, they just exchanged gifts." A half smile came and went quickly before Grice continued.

Iris eyed him skeptically as Grice continued, "Others have suggested it's a product of time travel. Our own future descendants went back to colonial times to correct a flaw in our governmental system—some future threat to our nation—that goes terribly wrong in their time."

Iris raised an eyebrow.

"The truth is, we don't know. Whatever its origin, its effects are real. You've seen that yourselves. And that's just scratching the surface," Nathan said.

Jackson struggled to grasp the concept. "So, we're dealing with something that has the power to reshape our country—our lives—and we don't even understand what it is, let alone how it works?"

"Welcome to the world of the Wardens," Nathan replied with a grim smile. "Our job isn't to understand it. It's to protect it. And right now, we need to keep it out of the Horsemen's hands at all costs."

Grice nodded. "Which is why we need to stop them. The Cassandra Collective might have its differences with the Wardens, but we recognize the danger of any one group having that much power."

"And we do know one thing," Nathan said, his eyes darkening, "they're waiting for the perfect moment. And that moment is fast approaching."

Grice nodded. "We believe they might be planning to use the Seal during the upcoming State of the Union address."

Jackson's stomach dropped. "That soon?"

"Yes," Nathan said, his voice filled with urgency. "So, we need to move quickly."

The weight of their mission hung over them. The fate of the country—and everything they held dear—was on the line.

"All right," Jackson said, his voice steady despite the storm inside him. "Let's get to work."

FIVE

The pre-dawn light through the cabin windows casts everything in a muted haze. Jackson stood by the fireplace, gripping a cup of coffee that had long since gone cold. His thoughts churned. The revelations from the night before shattered everything he believed—about his life, his family, and the very history of America.

Around the cabin, the others were scattered in various states of focus. Arjun, hunched over his laptop, had dark circles under his eyes illuminated by the screen. Grice paced by the window, his usual arrogance replaced with a sharp, restless energy. At the table, Nathan—Dad, Jackson reminded himself—sat with Grice, poring over documents that looked ancient.

The floor creaked, and Jackson turned to see Iris approaching. With concern etched on her face, she placed a gentle hand on his arm. "How are you doing?"

Jackson sighed and met her gaze. "Honestly? I don't

know. Everything's flipped upside down. I can't believe all this was going on right under our noses. My father... the Seal... the Horsemen." He shook his head as frustration bubbled to the surface. "How did we miss it?"

Iris squeezed his arm. Her touch was a quiet reassurance. "We weren't looking for it. We thought we were chasing history, not...living it."

Jackson's voice dropped to a whisper. "Now we're all that stands between the Horsemen and the destruction of the government. How are we supposed to handle that? We're historians, not spies."

Iris smiled faintly, though tension lingered in her eyes. "We'll figure it out. We have to."

Jackson looked at her. A spark of hope kindled inside him despite the overwhelming doubt that threatened to swallow him whole. He opened his mouth to speak, but before he could say anything, Nathan's voice cut through the room.

"All right, everyone. We need to finalize our plan. Time isn't on our side."

Jackson straightened, pulling himself together. Whatever doubts he had, there was no turning back now.

Arjun's voice broke the silence. "I think I've found something." Everyone gathered around as Arjun spun his laptop toward the center of the table. "I've been cross-referencing Margaret's notes with some encrypted chatter. I believe I've narrowed down the Horsemen's base."

Nathan leaned in, furrowing his brow. "Where?"

Arjun pulled up a map. "An abandoned military complex in the Adirondacks. It's been off the grid for years, but there has been a spike in power usage and supply deliveries lately."

Grice nodded. "That fits with the intel my team has gathered."

Jackson stared at the screen in disbelief. "So, what now?"

Nathan gave Jackson a steady look. "We need to infiltrate it." Before he could delve into the details, a knock at the door silenced the room. Everyone tensed. Jackson's hand instinctively moved toward the gun he'd been carrying. Nathan approached the door cautiously, gesturing for the others to stay back.

"Were you expecting anyone else?" Jackson whispered.

His father shook his head, tension visible in every line of his body.

When he opened the door, Thomas Crane stood on the threshold, brushing snow from his coat. "I have news," he said, stepping inside. "The Horsemen have accelerated their plans."

A flurry of questions erupted, but Crane raised his hand to quiet them. "They're no longer waiting for the State of the Union address. My sources say they plan to activate the Seal within the next forty-eight hours."

The blood drained from Jackson's face. "What? Why?"

"New information about the Seal's power," Crane explained, his expression grave. "There's a celestial alignment happening in two days, and the Horsemen believe it might amplify the Seal's effects."

Jackson shook his head in disbelief. "They're acting on superstition?"

Crane's serious expression made it clear that the situation was anything but trivial. "They think it's more than superstition. The alignment peaks at 11:11 PM, two days from now. They're calling it the 'Founders' Hour,' a nod to the Seal's origins."

Arjun, who had been typing intensely, looked up from his laptop with a frown. "He's right. There is a rare planetary alignment occurring that night. It happens once every few centuries. But how it relates to the Seal is another question."

Jackson smirked. "Sounds to me like a stab in the dark."

Iris stepped forward, her eyes narrowing. "Maybe so, but can we count on that?"

Nathan's expression hardened. "No. As long as they have the Seal, we can't take any chances. We need to adjust our plan—fast. Grice, can your team get the equipment and credentials we need in twenty-four hours?"

Grice nodded and began pulling out his phone. "I'll make some calls." He stepped into the next room, speaking in muted tones as he coordinated with his contacts.

Nathan turned to Arjun. "I need you to dig deeper into the military complex. Identify every entry point and every security measure. See how this celestial alignment could give the Horsemen an advantage with the Seal."

"On it," Arjun replied, typing rapidly.

Nathan's attention shifted to Jackson and Iris. "You two will go in undercover as potential recruits. Crane and I will brief you on what to expect."

Iris stiffened. "We can't. Margaret knows us."

Nathan grimaced. "Right. You'll need a different approach."

Grice returned, slipping his phone into his coat. "We can use my operatives. We will pose Jackson and Iris as intermediaries looking to broker a potential alliance with the Horsemen."

Jackson's eyebrows shot up. "An alliance? Why would they even want one?"

"There are rumors," Crane interjected. "Some factions within the Horsemen would like to expand their influence. An alliance could tempt them."

"It's risky," Nathan said, "but it's our best shot."

Grice grinned. "Leave the details to me. I'll get my team to craft the backstory and create credentials that keep your surface identity as far as Margaret knows, but we'll expunge anything that links Jackson to you. We'll edit your digital footprints—everything."

Nathan looked grimly at Grice. "Your team... Can we trust them?"

Grice met his gaze head-on. "I trust them, and you'll have to trust me."

Jackson watched his father silently weigh the options. "Okay."

Iris turned to Grice. "How long will it take?" Her voice was tense.

"Preliminary identities can be ready in hours. The full backstory will be done by tomorrow," Grice assured her.

Nathan nodded. "Good. You two will need to master the basics of the Collective and the Wardens. You need to know enough to be convincing without revealing any real secrets."

Jackson exchanged a glance with Iris. "What's our goal once we're inside?"

"Gather intelligence," Nathan replied. "Confirm the Seal's location and their activation plan. If possible, secure the Seal or sabotage their efforts."

Jackson's eyes narrowed. "That's a pretty tall order considering the fact that they're highly unlikely to leave us alone. And they're sure as hell not going to show us their secret operations."

Iris was silent, no doubt having similar concerns.

"And if we get caught?" Jackson asked.

Nathan's face darkened as he turned to Arjun. "Get together with Grice and work out some coms." Turning back to Jackson, he said, "We'll initiate a diversion to give you a chance to escape."

"What sort of diversion?" Jackson asked.

Nathan looked frankly at Jackson. "One we haven't figured out yet."

Jackson didn't like the sound of that, but he nodded. "Great. Let's get to work."

Hours passed in a blur of planning. Jackson and Iris pored over the details of their cover story, absorbing information about the Collective and the Horsemen and linking it all to an innocuous-sounding history research project. Every detail had to be perfect. One mistake and everything could fall apart.

As the sun dipped below the horizon, long shadows crept over the snow-blanketed landscape. Nathan called for a break, and Jackson stepped out onto the porch to get some fresh air. Iris joined him, shivering in the cold.

"You okay?" she asked.

Jackson chuckled bitterly. "A week ago, I was grading papers in elbow-patched tweed. Now we're about to infiltrate a secret society."

Iris smiled, though the tension remained in her eyes. "Yeah, I must have cut class the day they covered that in grad school."

He turned to face her, the weight of the mission hanging between them. "Can we really pull this off?"

Iris locked eyes with him, her expression firm. "Yes."

Jackson grinned, teasing her. "You're a terrible liar."

Iris readily agreed. "But I'd better get good at it by tomorrow."

Without thinking, Jackson pulled her into his arms. The cold faded as she pressed closer, her breath warm against his cheek. He kissed her, and the stress of the day slipped away for a moment.

When they pulled apart, Iris smiled softly. "Let's go save the world." She turned toward the door, then turned back. "But first, would you do that again?"

Jackson gladly complied.

BACK INSIDE, the fire crackled softly as the team resumed their work. Nathan stood by the mantel, staring into the flames.

Jackson approached him and quietly asked, "What about you? What will you be doing?"

Without turning from the fire, Nathan replied, "I'll be guiding you from here. My face is too recognizable to go into the field, but I'll be with you every step of the way."

Jackson hesitated. "Dad...all those years. Was it all for this?"

Nathan's shoulders sagged as he turned to face his son. "Not everything. But yes, much of my life has been in service to this mission. But I'm sorry for the pain I caused you."

Jackson swallowed hard, emotion rising in his chest. "I'm not sure I can forgive you, but I understand why you did it."

Nathan clasped his shoulder, his grip firm. "That's enough for now."

SIX

The rustic cabin beams loomed over Arjun's makeshift command center in a striking juxtaposition of old and new as his fingers flew across the keyboard. Jackson, Iris, and Crane stood huddled behind him in the dim light of the cabin's living room.

"If there's a digital trail, I'll find it," Arjun muttered, eyes locked on the screen. "Every thief leaves footprints —even the Horsemen."

Jackson leaned closer, trying to make sense of the rapid-fire code scrolling across the screen. "What exactly are we looking for?"

Arjun paused, fingers hovering above the keyboard. "Anything out of place. Spikes in data transfers, encrypted messages, or unusual access patterns. The Seal's theft would've left ripples in the digital world."

As he spoke, one of the screens flashed red. Arjun's eyes widened. "There! A burst of encrypted data was sent from the Heritage Center's network minutes before the alarm went off."

Iris edged closer, her arm brushing against Jackson's. "Can you decrypt it?" she asked, her voice filled with hope.

As he worked, Arjun's eyebrows furrowed while lines of code reflected off his glasses. After several tense minutes, he leaned back, frustration flickering across his face. "It's...complex. Quantum encryption layered with historical ciphers." He stared at the screen and then shook his head. "It's beyond my expertise."

The room went dead quiet. They'd been counting on Arjun for this breakthrough. Jackson raked a hand through his hair, feeling the weight of impending failure.

Crane, who had been silent until then, cleared his throat. "I know someone who might help—a cryptographer. She's brilliant but...particular about her clients."

Jackson turned to him, suspicion edging his voice. "Can we trust her?"

Crane met his gaze evenly. "With our lives. Her name's Claire. I'll give her a call."

As Crane stepped outside, Jackson turned to Iris. "What do you think?"

Iris crossed her arms and winced. "It's a gamble. I mean..." She leaned closer and spoke in a hushed voice. "Crane's a bit of a Luddite, so his idea of a cryptographer might be someone who uses 'password' as their password."

Arjun suppressed a laugh as Crane came back inside and said, "She's in."

IN THE EVENING, Jackson spotted Iris on the porch and went outside to join her. As he laced his fingers through hers, he gazed at the sunset. "There are moments when I just want to grab you and disappear—run away to a beach somewhere far from all this." He asked softly, "Would you come with me?"

Iris squeezed his hand, a smile tugging at her lips. "I'll go pack. Where are we going—so I know what to take."

Jackson wrapped his arms around her and looked out at the snow. "Somewhere warm."

"With a beach?" she asked, her excitement growing.

"Absolutely!"

Iris smiled wider. "And one of those huts on a pier over the water?"

Just thinking about it made Jackson feel warmer. "And a bottle of bubbly on ice."

Iris sighed dreamily as she gazed into his eyes.

Jackson inwardly groaned. "But for now, we'll have to settle for that pot of bitter canned coffee inside."

Iris leaned into his chest for a moment, then lifted her face, took a deep breath, and smirked. "Yum."

A FEW HOURS LATER, Jackson stood at the small train station near the cabin, waiting for their new ally. The Adirondack train pulled in, its bell cutting through the crisp mountain air. A woman in her midtwenties with sharp green eyes and a mass of curly red hair stepped off.

"Claire?" Jackson called out, stepping toward her.

She turned. Her eyes scanned him with curiosity. Her youth belied the intensity of her gaze. "You must be Jackson. Crane said you'd pick me up."

On the drive back to the cabin, Jackson filled her in on the situation. Claire listened, nodding occasionally. Her sharp questions revealed a keen understanding of both history and technology.

"So, this Arjun," Claire said, an edge of challenge in her voice. "Crane says he's good. But how good?"

Jackson glanced at her, gauging her tone. "The best. But this encryption is beyond anything we've ever seen."

Claire's eyes gleamed with determination. "Well, we'll see about that."

Back at the cabin, Claire dropped her bag and strode into the living room. She spotted Arjun hunched over his setup. "So," she said, her tone teasing but firm, "you're the tech wizard who couldn't crack it?"

Arjun straightened, meeting her gaze with a challenge of his own. "Given time, I would have."

"Time we don't have," Claire countered, shrugging off her jacket as she moved closer. "Show me what you've got."

The room seemed to hum with tension as Arjun pulled up the encrypted data. Claire leaned in, their shoulders brushing slightly, her focus locked on the glowing screen.

"Interesting," she murmured, her fingers hovering just above the keyboard. "It's a multi-layered encryption. Quantum-resistant algorithms with... Wait, is that a historical cipher?"

Jackson perked up. "Historical?"

Claire nodded, her fingers flying across the keys. "Yeah. It looks like they've woven in elements of an old cipher. But I can't quite make it out."

Arjun glanced at her, the competitive fire in his eyes softening. "It looks familiar... Something used by the Culper Ring, maybe."

Jackson's eyes widened. "The Culper Ring? The Revolutionary War spy network?"

Claire grinned, clearly impressed. "Combining cutting-edge tech with historical techniques. Smart. This is going to be fun."

※

Hours passed as Arjun and Claire worked side by side, their initial rivalry giving way to collaboration. The technical jargon flew between them, leaving the others in the room in varying states of confusion.

"Look at this sequence," Claire said, pointing to a string of characters. "They've twisted the Vigenère cipher into something new."

Arjun's eyes lit up as he leaned closer. "Using the cipher as a key for the quantum encryption. It's genius."

As the night wore on, the rest of the group settled into a quiet routine while the two cryptographers kept working.

Iris leaned toward Jackson, nodding toward the pair. "Looks like they're bonding."

Jackson smirked. "They grow up so fast."

While Claire and Arjun debated their next move, Jackson and Iris slipped outside onto the porch. The cool night air wrapped around them, crisp and refreshing—a welcome reprieve from the intensity indoors.

Iris leaned against the railing and gazed at the dark expanse of trees. "It feels like we're in way over our heads."

Jackson stepped closer, his fingers brushing hers before settling on the railing. "I know," he said quietly. "But I believe in this team. We'll figure it out."

She turned to him, her eyes searching his face, looking for something—reassurance, perhaps, or clarity. "Do you ever wonder if we're doing the right thing?"

A faint smile tugged at his lips. "No," he said. "But I constantly wonder if we're doing it the right way."

Iris felt her heart skip as she considered his words. She wanted to offer something encouraging, but the words didn't come.

Instead, Jackson leaned in, his lips brushing against hers in a soft, tender kiss. It was fleeting, yet full of meaning—a momentary escape from the danger shadowing their every step.

She could live on moments like these.

Their kiss broke with the sound of Claire's voice echoing from inside. Iris grimaced. "What's that you said about running away?"

Jackson chuckled, pulling Iris closer. "Don't tempt me."

Iris shivered. "Until then, we should probably go back inside before we ruin everything by freezing out here."

※

Inside, they found Claire and Arjun hunched over their computers, deeply absorbed in their work. The rest of the cabin was quiet, the others having found places to grab a few hours of sleep.

Iris pulled out her phone and scrolled through her email, stopping at a message about a university job she'd applied for—a beautifully worded rejection. That world now seemed so far away that it barely mattered anymore. She slipped her phone back into her pocket.

Suddenly, Claire's voice pierced the silence. "Holy crap!"

Alarmed, Jackson and Iris sprang to their feet.

"What? What happened?" Iris asked, looking around for signs of danger.

"We cracked it!" Claire exclaimed, turning to Arjun with a wide grin. She practically threw herself into his arms before they both awkwardly pulled away with a chuckle.

The team gathered around as Claire pulled up the decrypted message on the screen. Hoarse from hours of work, she said, "The message contained coordinates. It's—"

"Wall Street," Arjun finished, staring at the screen. "They're targeting the financial system."

Jackson's phone buzzed, and he paled as he checked the news. "Everyone, look at this."

He held up his phone, and the others crowded around. Headlines flashed across the screen.

"NYSE HALTS ALL TRADING"

"GLOBAL MARKETS IN FREEFALL"

"WALL STREET IN CHAOS"

"It's already happening." Iris's voice was barely above a whisper.

Jackson rubbed his temples. The headlines blurred together. "We're too late."

Arjun leaned back from the table. "The crash caused a ripple effect—banks are freezing transactions. Supply chains are disrupted. People are panicking."

Grice stepped forward. His face was tight with worry. "They're not just disabling systems. They're controlling them."

"But why the financial markets?" Iris asked. "What's their endgame?"

"Power," Jackson replied darkly. "The kind the Founding Fathers feared most."

"Exactly," Iris interjected. "Chaos makes people vulnerable and easier to control."

"But this wasn't their endgame—it was a proof of concept," Claire added.

Jackson's jaw tightened. "Then we use this to predict their next move. If Wall Street was the beginning, what's the logical escalation?"

"Energy grids," Arjun said, pulling up a map. "Or communications networks. Anything that amplifies chaos on a national scale."

The room went silent as the team processed the gravity of the situation. Arjun and Claire exchanged a glance. Their earlier rivalry was now replaced by mutual respect.

"This isn't over," Jackson said firmly. "We know what they're capable of now. And we know where to strike next."

"The Federal Reserve," Iris murmured. "If they're attacking Wall Street..."

"They'll go after the entire financial system next," Jackson finished. "We have to be ready."

As dawn broke, the first rays of sunlight streamed through the windows, casting shadows across the floor. The magnitude of what lay ahead loomed over them, but in that light, they found a glimmer of hope. Their team was stronger than before, and they were ready to face whatever came next.

SEVEN

Watching the stars while Rome burns? Iris read aloud from her phone, her voice tight with frustration. The message had arrived moments after the market crash, its timing as precise as the chaos it mocked.

Jackson paced the cabin's main room, the morning light casting long shadows through the windows. "They played us. That whole celestial alignment bull—"

"Was exactly what they wanted us to focus on," Crane finished, his calm demeanor cracking. He stood by the fireplace, where days ago, they'd discussed the very event that never happened.

Claire, eyes glued to her laptop, looked up. "The encryption we broke—it wasn't just a victory message. There's more." Her fingers moved rapidly over the keyboard as Arjun leaned closer. "It's layered, just like before, but this time..."

"This time, we know what to look for," Arjun

finished, locking eyes with her for a moment until Crane cleared his throat, pulling them back.

Crane turned to the group, his expression grim. "It's time you knew the full story. The Wardens—and the Horsemen—go back much further than you realize. Their ultimate goal isn't just the market crash. That was only the beginning."

Jackson stopped pacing and moved closer to Iris. "Tell us everything."

Crane glanced at Nathan, who nodded in agreement. Settling into one of the worn leather chairs, Crane flexed his weathered hands and drew a deep breath. "The Wardens weren't just formed to protect artifacts like the Seal. We were created to preserve democracy itself."

As Crane spoke, snowflakes began falling outside the cabin windows. A winter storm was rolling in.

"What most people don't realize," Crane continued, "is that the Founding Fathers faced threats beyond British control. There were powerful factions that viewed America's formation as an opportunity to create something very different from democracy."

A log shifted in the fireplace, sending sparks up the chimney. Outside, the snow fell harder, adding to the cabin's isolation.

"The Horsemen go back before the revolution?" Iris asked with her historian's mind racing.

"They went by a different name then, but their goal was the same," Crane explained. "They used chaos as a weapon to take control of governmental power. They've adapted their methods over time, but their mission hasn't changed."

Claire looked up from her screen. "Their encryption—it's not just complex. It's evolved. Like it's been refined over centuries."

"Exactly," Crane said. "The Wardens—the true Wardens—were formed in response to guard the principles of democracy. Your family," he said, looking at Jackson, "has been part of that fight since the beginning."

Iris glanced at Jackson. This man who'd made a career of studying history suddenly found himself part of it.

"My father," Jackson began.

"Knew the stakes," Nathan said, finishing his thought. "As did my father before me. But it's time you understood why we've all been involved."

Crane continued, "Margaret was meant to be the next generation's guardian."

"Until she switched sides," Iris added, confusion clouding her face.

"But did she?" Claire's voice was soft, yet it drew everyone's attention. "The message we decrypted—it's strange. The text almost seems..."

"Like it's meant for two audiences," Arjun interjected, moving closer to Claire's screen. He squinted at the code.

Crane nodded slowly. "Margaret's actions might not be what they appear. But for now, we need to focus on the Horsemen's real plan."

"Hold on," Iris said a bit more forcefully than she'd intended. "You can't just drop something like that and go on."

But Crane did. "The market crash wasn't just about money. It's about instability—fear—chaos that makes people accept solutions they'd normally reject."

"Social engineering through economic terrorism," Iris murmured, sensing Jackson tense beside her.

"But why now?" Jackson asked. "If they've been working toward this for centuries, why suddenly ramp things up now?"

Crane stoked the fire. "They've never been this close before. Their influence has spread through the private sector and beyond to the government."

"A divided society," Iris said, her research clicking into place. "Political polarization, economic uncertainty, social media…"

"And the Seal," Jackson finished.

"A perfect storm," Claire said, looking up from her laptop. "They don't need to create chaos. They just need to amplify it."

Crane nodded grimly. "And with the Seal's power, they can disable or activate any system they want. Imagine power grids failing, communication networks going dark, and transportation systems crashing—all without knowing the cause."

Jackson's face tightened. "Create a groundswell of panic, then position themselves as the solution."

It nearly took Iris's breath away. "A solution that would reshape America."

"They call it 'managed democracy,'" Crane explained. "A system where everyone supposedly has an equal voice."

"But some voices are more equal than others," Iris said, her tone dark.

Outside, the snow thickened, blanketing the cabin in a quiet, oppressive white. The team sat in silence, absorbing the enormity of what they had learned. Claire's laptop pinged, signaling another decrypted message.

"Oh God," she whispered.

Arjun leaned in, his face paling as he scanned the screen.

"What is it?" Jackson demanded.

Arjun looked up at Crane. "You were right. The market crash wasn't just their opening move. It was a test. And now..."

"Now they know exactly what they can do," Claire finished. "And they're ready for phase two."

The fire crackled, its warmth doing nothing to dispel the chill that had settled over the group. Outside, the storm raged, but the real tempest was yet to come.

"Phase two?" Jackson's voice was low, though he already suspected the answer.

Arjun and Claire exchanged a glance before Arjun spoke. "They're calling it 'Cascade Protocol.' That's all we know."

Jackson's expression darkened. "It's enough, though. They've already manipulated the market. What's next? Energy? Transportation?"

Iris felt a wave of disbelief wash over her as she pulled away from Jackson. Moving to the cabin's wall of bookshelves, she pulled out a leather-bound book. "It's happened before," she said. "During the Great Depression—"

"They tried to exploit the panic." Crane nodded. "But the Wardens stopped them."

"The Wardens?" Jackson said quietly. "So, my grandfather—he wasn't just researching the Depression, was he?"

"He helped prevent a coup," Nathan confirmed. "A coup that would have replaced democracy with 'managed stability.'"

Iris stared out at the snowstorm, watching as it sealed them in. The fire crackled louder, sending sparks upward. "Back then, they failed. But this time, they have the Seal."

"And technology," Arjun added. "Not to mention social media, which can spread panic in minutes."

"If they control digital systems," Claire said, her voice grim, "that includes traffic lights, power grids, supply chains—everything that makes our lives...livable. Unless you live on an off-the-grid homestead."

As they took turns outlining the impending disaster, Nathan spoke firmly, "We know what we're facing, so let's focus."

Before he could finish, the power went out, plunging the cabin into near darkness. The faint light of afternoon filtered through the frost on the windows.

A half-hour later, the lights came back on, and

Jackson returned from outside, stomping snow from his boots. "Where were we?"

"We were wondering how much fuel is left in the generator," Iris said, pulling her coat tighter.

Jackson shrugged. "Dad, what do you think? Enough propane to last the night?"

Nathan shrugged. "Easily. It's a five-hundred-gallon tank, so we're good for at least a week."

"Bigger problem," Arjun added, lifting his hand. "The internet's out, too."

Claire rubbed her forehead, elbows resting on the table.

Nathan stood. "This is a setback, but we'll deal with it. We're all running on fumes. Let's use this as a chance to rest. In an hour, we'll shut down the generator to give it a rest, keep the wood stove burning, and get some sleep. We'll take shifts overnight to keep watch."

At dawn, Jackson fired up the generator, and the team got back to work. The internet was still down, but Claire had managed to download some encrypted files before losing the connection.

"Got something," Arjun said, his eyes narrowing. "We've picked up chatter on the ham radio. Banks across the country are reporting system failures. Locks, safes...everything's glitching."

"They're moving faster than we thought," Grice said, his voice heavy.

Claire looked up from the files she'd been studying. "Wait—I've been trying to find a pattern, but there isn't one. It's erratic, as if the Seal's power doesn't always behave as intended. You can't fully control it, which, more importantly, means they can't fully control it either."

The lights flickered again, and the generator sputtered out.

"We shouldn't have run out of fuel yet," Jackson said as he moved to the window. Through the swirling snow, he spotted movement. "Two snowmobiles. They've found us."

"And drained our propane tank," Nathan added.

"They tracked our decryption attempts," Arjun said, wiping his hard drives.

"But in theory…"

"No time for theory," Crane warned, checking his weapon. "We need to move. Now."

"Move where? We're snowed in," Grice muttered.

As they gathered essentials, Claire's laptop displayed one final decoded message before she closed the lid.

FEDERAL RESERVE

EIGHT

"Two snowmobiles approaching from the north," Crane reported from his position at the window. "Three riders minimum."

Nathan was already moving. "Everyone grab only what's essential. Jackson, help me with the cellar door."

As the others scrambled to gather equipment, Jackson followed his father to the kitchen pantry. Inside, Nathan pressed against one of the panels to reveal a concealed latch. The wall swung inward, exposing stone steps descending into darkness.

"This tunnel leads to the equipment shed," Nathan explained, his voice quiet and urgent. "My old Hummer's parked there."

"A Hummer?" Arjun asked, already stuffing his laptop into his backpack. "Are you sure it can drive through two feet of snow?"

While he gathered supplies, Nathan said, "No." He

paused long enough to look directly at Jackson. "Got a better idea?"

"Well, no."

"Then let's go."

Claire was hastily disconnecting hard drives when her laptop pinged with a final message. "Wait— Cascade Protocol... It's—"

The distinctive whine of snowmobile engines grew louder.

"Grab it and go," Jackson ordered, helping Iris gather the most crucial historical documents. The leather-bound volumes felt heavy—laden with secrets of the past—as he shoved them into her bag.

She shot him a tense look. "The archivist in me is cringing."

"I'd ignore her and listen to the survivor in you," Jackson murmured with a smirk.

Iris's lips curved in a fleeting smile.

The snowmobile engines cut out abruptly, and Jackson's heart tightened.

"They're dismounting," Grice warned, moving away from the window. "Two minutes, maybe less."

Nathan flicked on a flashlight and led them down the stone steps. Jackson took the rear position, easing the hidden door closed behind them with a soft click and sealing off the only barrier between them and the Horsemen.

The tunnel was more modern than Jackson expected. It was built from a large culvert with flat floorboards laid down for walking.

"I like what you've done with the place," Jackson muttered to his father.

Nathan smirked. "Lesson one: plan ahead."

A muffled crash echoed from above. The Horsemen had breached the cabin.

"How much further?" Iris asked. Her tone was calm in spite of the tension around them.

"About two hundred yards," Nathan said.

Claire trailed behind Arjun, laptop in one arm while she typed with the other. Her foot caught on a loose board, and she tripped.

Arjun caught her and helped her along. "For God's sake, Claire. Can you put that away for one minute?"

"But I need five. I've got to decode Cascade Protocol. It's not just about banks. It's—"

Another crash sounded, closer this time, shaking dust from the tunnel ceiling. "They're searching for the entrance," Crane whispered. "It won't take long to find it."

Claire, still glued to her screen, looked up sharply. "Cascade Protocol is a sequence. The market crash was only the first step. They're planning to trigger systematic failures across the country."

The security door to the equipment shed loomed ahead. Nathan punched in a code on a keypad beside the solid steel barrier, but the display remained dark. "Still no power."

Jackson stepped forward to help. "Can we open it manually?"

"There's a mechanical override, but it'll make

noise," Nathan warned, wrenching a metal panel off the wall to reveal a hand crank.

More gunfire sounded above. The walls groaned as if echoing their urgency.

"They've found the entrance," Crane said. His tone was edged with warning. "We've got less than a minute."

Jackson and Nathan worked the crank. The metal groaned as it gave way, filling the tunnel with a sound that made everyone flinch. As soon as the gap was wide enough, Iris and Claire squeezed through, followed by Arjun and Grice.

Footsteps thundered behind them.

"They're in the tunnel," Grice announced as he helped Nathan slam the door shut behind them.

"Won't hold them long," Nathan said, already moving ahead. "But it'll buy us time."

They scrambled up the stairs, their flashlight beams dancing across the metal walls. Claire clutched her laptop like a lifeline.

"The market crash," she gasped between breaths, "was a test. Now they're planning to shut down everything—transportation, communication networks, energy grids—"

"Save it for later," Arjun said, urging her forward.

At the top of the stairs, the Hummer sat, massive and ready. Through two small garage door windows, Jackson spotted two more snowmobiles circling the clearing.

"They've flanked us," Grice muttered, his gun ready.

"The Hummer can outrun them," Nathan said, his voice confident but edged with doubt. "If it starts."

Iris turned to Nathan in silent alarm.

"If they can use the Seal to cause a power outage, it might interfere with machines," Nathan said.

"What?" Jackson shot his father a shocked look.

Nathan urged Jackson into the driver's seat. "Plus, this thing's twenty years old, so..."

"So, we might not even get it running?" Iris asked. Her voice was sharp.

Another metallic boom reverberated through the tunnel. The security door had given way.

Teeth clenched, Jackson checked his weapon and scanned the controls on the dashboard. "Dad, you know the terrain. Once we're on our way down the road, where do we go?"

"East service road," Nathan replied, not missing a beat. "Higher ground, less snow. If we can clear the ridge—"

A shot was fired. One of the Horsemen was in the equipment shed. Crane opened his window and fired. Iris stared at the fallen man until Jackson grabbed her and pulled her into the Hummer.

Snow sprayed through the gaps in the shed as the remaining team members clambered into the Hummer.

"Is everyone in?" Jackson asked. He started to get out to open the garage door, but Nathan pulled him back. "No, just drive through it."

Closing his driver's side door, Jackson started the Hummer. Nothing happened. No one spoke. Jackson tried again. Iris locked eyes with one of the Horsemen as he looked through the window. Time slowed as the Horseman raised his weapon.

A single gunshot rang out, shattering a shed window and hitting the driver's side mirror. The engine coughed, sputtered, then roared to life.

"Move!" Nathan yelled as Jackson turned the key.

Jackson wasted no time slamming down the gas. The Hummer tore through the shed door with a spray of snow, ice, and wood splinters.

The snowmobiles roared in pursuit, cutting through the clearing to catch up.

"Hold on!" Jackson called as they hit the service road. The Hummer fishtailed before its massive tires gripped the icy ground.

Iris braced herself against the door, watching the Horsemen close the distance between them. "They're gaining!"

Jackson gripped the wheel tighter. "Trust me. We'll lose them."

Nathan leaned forward, his eyes wide. "There's a fork up ahead. Can we split them off?"

Jackson's eyes narrowed, calculating. "Hang on tight."

The Hummer surged forward, barreling down the narrow trail. Jackson veered sharply right at the fork, causing two of the snowmobiles to skid and miss the turn.

Grice leaned out and fired a shot that echoed over the snow. One snowmobile pulled back, but the last one stayed hot on their trail.

Hitting the gas, Jackson sped over rough terrain while the Hummer jostled as they climbed the ridge. The last snowmobile struggled, slowing as they pulled further away.

"Not much farther," Nathan said, his voice steady. "If we can clear this ridge, we've got a chance."

As they crested the final rise, the last of the Horsemen vanished into the haze behind them. Silence fell over the Hummer as Nathan slowed, taking a winding road that led them farther from danger.

Beneath a dense cover of trees, Jackson slowed down.

Nathan turned. His expression was somber. "They're not giving up. This was just a preview."

Jackson glanced through the mirror at Iris. Her face was resolute despite the fear in her eyes.

"You okay?"

"Yeah."

His heart pounded as he saw something different in her—a resolve that mirrored his own. In that quiet moment, they'd crossed not just the ridge but a threshold within themselves. Whatever lay ahead, they were bound by more than just circumstance.

NINE

"Hang on!" Jackson called out as the Hummer's engine sputtered. He pulled off the road, over rough terrain, and into a wooded area. With one last cough, the engine fell silent, leaving only Jackson's frustrated sigh. Snow flew fast, covering the edges of the road and muffling every sound beyond their cramped space in the vehicle.

"The transmission's done," Jackson said, gripping the wheel as if he could coax the vehicle back to life. "This storm just made sure of it."

Crane, sitting in the back, scanned the area as best he could. "We're too exposed. If they find us here, we'll be cornered."

Nathan nodded, making a quick decision. "Everyone grab some branches and snow to help hide the Hummer as much as we can. Then we'll take what we can carry and head for the main road. Let's just hope the storm covers our tracks."

The team gathered their most essential gear and prepared to leave when a faint, droning hum interrupted the howling wind. Jackson's body tensed as he turned his head, straining to catch the sound. Snowmobiles.

He looked at Nathan, whose expression was set in grim determination.

"They're coming," Jackson murmured. "And they're close. Let's head into the trees."

As they stepped out into the night, the storm whipped around them, quickly erasing their tracks in the swirling snow. Concealed by the trees and the blizzard conditions, the snowmobiles passed by them and continued down the road. The team pressed on in silence. Their breaths formed frosty clouds as they made their way through the trees parallel to the road. Few people remained on the road now. The only sound was their footsteps, muffled by the thickening snowfall.

Nearly an hour later, a distant glow appeared down the road. They arrived at a repair shop with a yard filled with old cars, riding lawnmowers, tractors, and other machines, many of which had been gutted for parts. Inside, a grizzled elderly man sat surrounded by a disassembled snowblower and a few scattered tools.

While the others gathered around an old kerosene space heater, Jackson approached the owner, who greeted him with a nod.

"What brings you out here in this storm?" the man asked.

Jackson managed a tired smile. "Our car died a ways back. We're looking for something snow-ready."

The owner nodded knowingly. "Got a truck out back—solid, full tank, just tuned up. Cash only."

Jackson handed over a wad of bills.

The owner pocketed the money and gestured toward the truck. "She'll get you where you need to go."

A FEW MILES down the road, they found a diner—a warm and inviting refuge in the otherwise desolate village center. As they stepped inside, they shivered as the heavy door closed behind them, sealing out the biting wind and snow. The comforting aroma of coffee and bacon wafted from the kitchen as the team made their way to a table at the far end, shedding their coats and settling into the vinyl-cushioned chrome chairs.

A waitress approached with a knowing smile, setting down mugs of steaming coffee before each of them without waiting for an order. "Looks like you could use something warm."

Jackson cupped his hands around his mug, feeling the heat seep into his frozen fingers as he surveyed the group. Despite their exhaustion, a quiet strength seemed to settle among them. The knowledge that they had made it this far added a flicker of resolve to each face.

Nathan was the first to break the silence. "We need

a new plan. With the Hummer down and that storm picking up, we're lucky we got here."

Grice leaned back, blowing on his coffee. "Right. But luck will only get us so far, and time's running out."

Claire nodded, setting down her cup with a faint clink. "I think I've finally located their base."

Grice stared in disbelief. "And you're just mentioning it now?"

Claire leaned back, her jaw dropped. "Oh, I mentioned it a lot while I was freezing my ass off in the back of the truck, and you were all cozy and warm in the cab."

Jackson averted his eyes from an indignant Grice and fixed his gaze on Claire. "So where is it?"

"I've got a general location, but I need to check a few things to narrow it down," she replied, glancing around. "Anyone see an electrical outlet?"

Arjun went to ask the waitress.

Minutes later, Arjun and Claire sat at a nearby table with their computers and phones plugged into a borrowed extension cord. They returned to the group with a laptop displaying a satellite map of the region.

Claire pointed and traced a path to a remote area in the northern mountain range. "I triangulated signals from their last known locations and narrowed it down to this place. There's an old military base on a mountaintop here. That's where they're operating from."

Jackson peered at the screen. "You're sure?"

Claire answered with a narrow-eyed stare.

"We're sure," Arjun added.

Nathan's jaw tightened as he studied the map. "I know those mountains. If they're set up out there, they've got plenty of cover."

Grice, who had been quiet, finally spoke up. "And we've got a rickety truck, no clue where the Seal is, and no knowledge of their security system."

Claire scowled at Grice for a moment, then explained slowly, "I'm not suggesting we Riverdance our way to the front door and knock. I'm just telling you that Arjun and I have located their base. Of course, we'll need more information. But for now, a simple thank you will do."

Jackson winced. The look of disdain on Claire's face was painful to see, even as an observer.

The waitress returned with their food. The simple meal lifted their spirits, and for a few moments, they set aside their differences and focused on the meal.

With tensions eased somewhat, Claire said, "Arjun and I will scour the public—and not-so-public—property records for building permits and blueprints. With any luck—and our skills—we'll be able to reverse engineer their security setup from the electrical schematic. We should have more details in a couple of hours."

Nathan turned to Crane. "And then what?"

Crane set his coffee cup down, his expression pensive. "An old-school stealth approach. In this weather, there's no way to get our hands on any sophisticated surveillance equipment. But we can start with a reconnaissance mission. The weather will work in our favor to conceal our approach. Then we'll work out a couple of contingencies depending on what we find there. From that point, the plan is simple—get in, gather intel, and get out. No unnecessary risks."

"But it is risky, no matter what," Grice muttered.

Iris looked down, her fingers tracing the rim of her coffee cup. "He's got a point. Even with the right intel and approach, we're still outnumbered. The Horsemen are organized, well-equipped, and they know the terrain."

Jackson reached across the table, giving her hand a reassuring squeeze. "But we're smart and resourceful—and we've got right on our side."

Iris winced. "History is riddled with cases of people who were in the right but had wrong results."

"We're not them." Jackson gave her a confident smile.

To his surprise, she smiled back, almost as if she believed him. "I'm sorry. It's all just a bit overwhelming."

"That's what planning is for—so we can let go of those feelings and get the job done."

They finished their meals and lingered at the table. Each person was lost in their own thoughts.

Crane broke the silence, his voice softened by the exhaustion etched on his face. "We've all had close calls and encountered things we didn't expect. But with a good plan and sharp wits, we'll succeed."

The waitress returned, topping off their coffee. As they murmured their thanks, Jackson looked around the table, contemplating their next move.

Claire closed her laptop. "Arjun and I will get to work on the compound."

Arjun studied her, his eyes lit with admiration, and he nodded.

Crane and Grice headed to a corner to make some phone calls to any contacts who might have knowledge of the Horsemen. Nathan, Jackson, and Iris discussed likely scenarios and roughed out some plans.

By the time they returned to their truck, the snow had let up. With Jackson at the wheel, Nathan and Crane got into the cab while the rest piled into the truck bed. The cold air bit their skin as they pulled onto the road and left the diner behind.

TEN

The snowfall had slowed to a light dusting as the group reached the outskirts of the mountains. Crane guided Nathan off the main road onto a narrow lane bordered by towering pines, and soon, they spotted the faint outline of a cabin nestled between snow-laden trees. A soft glow emanated from inside, hinting at warmth and shelter.

As they climbed out of the truck, Arjun raised his eyebrows and cast a skeptical glance at Crane. "I didn't know you were into rustic charm, Crane. Is this some kind of secret safe house?"

Crane, pulling his coat closer against the cold, cracked a grin. "Safe house? I wish. Our resources aren't quite that extensive. No...I had an associate book this through Airbnb."

The group stifled their laughter, the tension of the past hours easing in a rare moment of levity.

Iris shook her head with a smirk tugging at her lips. "Nice."

He shrugged, looking unapologetic. "Just because we're on the run doesn't mean we can't have running water and heat."

They stepped inside, grateful for the shelter. The cabin was small but cozy, furnished with a large leather couch, a set of plaid armchairs, and a compact but functional kitchen off to the side. A stack of firewood sat beside a stone fireplace, which Jackson wasted no time putting to use. Once lit and burning, the fire cast an amber glow over the space. Jackson stood by the fire and relaxed in its warmth for the first time in hours.

The group settled in, each finding a spot to unwind. Arjun and Claire immediately claimed the small table near the kitchen, where they set up their laptops and notes to work on the decoding. The rest of the team dispersed. Grice took over fire duty, feeding logs into the crackling flames while Nathan checked his gear with his expression pensive.

With the fire crackling away, the team unwound in their own ways. Claire and Arjun were still busy at the table, but laughter and quiet exchanges eased the tension that had dogged their journey until now.

Jackson sank onto the couch, and Iris joined him. Their shoulders brushed as they sat in silence, watching the fire. She glanced at him. His eyes were soft in the firelight.

"I have these moments when I think this can't be real."

He nodded with a faint smile touching his lips. "It feels surreal sometimes. And then there are moments like this—quiet, even peaceful."

Iris looked away. Her gaze was thoughtful. "Your father's pretty impressive, you know."

Jackson stared into the fire, brows furrowed. "Yeah, he is."

Across the room, Nathan's gaze rested on Jackson and Iris, and he smiled.

Iris put her hand on Jackson's. "Go talk to him."

He furrowed his eyebrows. "Why?"

"Because you can—and maybe should. And you never know when the next chance will be," Iris said simply.

Jackson continued to stare at the fire with a troubled expression. Moments later, without warning, he patted her knee, said, "Okay," and left her. Grabbing a kitchen chair, he went over and sat by his father. "How're you doing through all this?"

"I'm good." Nathan's eyes lit with a smile. "In a way, I'm more comfortable here than in real life." His smile faded. "At least I'm better at this. I never wanted it that way. It's just how things turned out. And I'm sorry."

The pained truth in his father's admission gripped Jackson in the gut. "I can see how you could get caught up in all this. It kind of takes over your life."

Nathan stared at the fire across the room. "It never took over my love for my family—for you. I just wanted to make the world a better place for you to grow up in."

"It's hard for a kid to understand that," Jackson said.

His father's eyes filled with pain. "I know. I think that's what weighs on me the most. I hurt you in ways that don't heal. I know it, and I can't undo it."

Jackson wanted to disagree, but he couldn't. "For what it's worth, I understand better now."

Nathan looked surprised. "Do you? I can't imagine that helps much."

Jackson lifted his shoulders. "It helps a little." The sad regret in his father's eyes overwhelmed him.

After a long silence stretched between them, Nathan said, "You should know..." He paused and swallowed. "I want you to know that I'm proud of the man you've become."

An odd mix of pride and emotions Jackson couldn't define caught in his throat. "Thanks, Dad."

They sat in silence until Nathan glanced across the room toward Iris. "I like Iris."

Jackson smiled. "Yeah, I do too."

Nathan placed a hand on his son's shoulder and gave it a firm squeeze. "If I were you, I wouldn't make her sit over there all alone."

Jackson grinned at his father and went back to Iris.

At the table, Arjun fidgeted, repositioning his computer while he stole a sidelong glance at Claire. The firelight cast a warm glow over her face as she focused on the strings of code running across her screen. Her brow was furrowed in concentration. After a moment, Arjun cleared his throat, mustering the courage to break the silence.

"So, um...this is a long time to be away."

She wrinkled her face. "From what?"

Arjun froze. "Uh...you know, from...work?"

"I've been freelancing, so this is my work." She turned back to her screen.

Arjun swallowed hard. "And—"

Claire turned and stared at him, not too patiently.

"From...you know, people."

"Yeah, I guess." Claire shrugged and returned to her work.

Arjun glanced about, searching for words. "It must be hard on relationships."

Looking nonplussed, Claire turned to face him. "Are you—"

"No. What? I was just—"

She looked at him frankly. "Wondering if I have a boyfriend?" She peered at him as if he were speaking in some sort of esoteric programming language.

Arjun took a moment, then blurted out, "Yes."

Claire blinked but smiled faintly. "Oh, then no."

"Oh."

She smirked. "A real shocker, right?"

"Well, yes." Her self-deprecation caught Arjun off guard. In every other way, she was confident. Nothing seemed to ruffle her—not even being chased by armed Horsemen.

Claire looked into his eyes with a softness that just

about did him in. "Thanks. It's uh… I don't date much." She stared at her keyboard. "Guys seem to find me off-putting."

"Right." He froze, then recovered. "I mean, you're not that at all. But I get what you mean." At that moment, he felt as if he'd broken through a brick wall of defense and made a connection with Claire.

A smile bloomed on her face, making Arjun feel as if the warmth of the sun had come out just for him.

"I get that not everyone finds all this tech stuff as fascinating as I do, but guys who do tend to find me… not as fascinating," Claire said.

Claire looked surprisingly vulnerable, and it took all of Arjun's willpower to resist drawing her into his arms. Instead, he said, "They're intimidated."

Claire nodded, the thought clearly having occurred to her, too. "I know I'm a little…intense."

Arjun grinned and might have nodded in agreement a little too enthusiastically, judging by her soft laugh. He hastened to add, "But I like that about you."

"Really?" Her eyes sparkled.

Arjun couldn't seem to stop staring. He knew his gaze was too deep and too long, but he couldn't help himself. He couldn't hide how he felt.

Claire held his gaze with a genuine smile. "You know what I like about you?"

Arjun hesitated, afraid of the answer.

"You," she said softly.

Arjun froze. Somewhere in his mind, a voice told

him that this was his moment—his chance to make some sort of move. And yet, he couldn't manage even a word.

"I like you," Claire added. She gazed into his eyes and leaned closer.

As if he'd been drawn into her magnetic field, he leaned closer to her. His eyes swept over her face. Her lips parted.

"How's it going?" Grice appeared out of nowhere and pulled up a chair.

With that, they were back at work as though nothing had changed. But it had.

ON THE OTHER side of the room, Jackson and Claire enjoyed a tranquil moment. She was glad he'd had a good talk with his father. With potential danger in their near future, she wanted them to clear the air. But with that done, her thoughts turned to her feelings for Jackson. "I'm sorry I've been a little on edge."

Jackson looked either kindly or genuinely surprised. She wasn't sure which, but she appreciated it either way.

Iris stared at the fire. "I've always liked the idea of grace under pressure. It's such an admirable way to be." She turned to Jackson. "And you're so good at it!"

Jackson shrugged the compliment off.

"And I'm not." She exhaled. "At all." She turned back to the fire.

Jackson touched her chin and gently turned her to face him. "I have no idea what you're talking about."

"Really?" Iris took a moment to absorb that new fact. "Because I feel like half the time I'm screaming inside like my hair's on fire, and the other half, I'm just paralyzed with fear."

Jackson wrapped his arms around her and held her against his warm, sturdy chest until she wished she could stay in that safety forever. When he finally released her, he smoothed some stray strands of hair from her forehead. "Everyone gets scared on the inside. It's what you do on the outside that counts. You're a rock." His eyes twinkled.

"That's the nicest thing anyone's ever said to me." She let out a soft laugh that took the tension she'd been bottling up with it.

For a long while, the cabin was quiet, save for the crackle of the fire and the steady clack of Claire's fingers on the keyboard. Just as everyone was settling into a rare sense of comfort, Arjun's head snapped up, his eyes sharp with a new intensity.

"Guys," he said, his voice breaking the peaceful lull. "I'm picking up something—movement near the compound."

The team went still, the atmosphere shifting in an instant. Jackson and Iris straightened, alert, while Grice set down the fire poker, his expression hardened.

"What kind of movement?" Nathan asked, moving closer to the table.

Arjun scanned the data quickly. "Security patterns, maybe. But whatever it is, it's more active than it should be at this hour."

ELEVEN

The early morning cast a pale light over the snow-covered hills as the team approached the Horsemen's compound, a small grouping of concrete buildings partially concealed by trees and a tall perimeter fence. Jackson scanned the area, his gaze sweeping over the snowy landscape to the guards on their rotation.

Claire crouched beside him, laptop in hand, still intercepting data from the Horsemen's local network. "It's odd," she murmured. "For all the noise they're making on a global level, their tech here looks practically archaic."

Jackson gave her a curious glance. "You're saying they don't have high-level security here?"

She nodded, tapping her screen. "Their internal surveillance is barely a step above standard CCTV. It's as if they've focused all their cyber resources elsewhere."

"Like on the Seal? Maybe they've figured out how

to leverage the Seal's power to execute their attacks," Arjun said.

Claire barely took her eyes off the screen. "If the Seal is channeling a broad enough cyberattack network to make them formidable globally, it might come at a cost to their local resources."

Iris looked over, intrigued. "So, you're saying they're so focused on the Seal that they're neglecting their own stronghold's protection?"

Claire tilted her head. "Not neglecting—just lacking. They might not have enough power left."

Crane shook his head in astonishment. "So, everything hinges on the Seal. Without that, they're no more than a ragtag militia."

"But a confident one," Grice added. "Rightly so, as long as they possess the Seal."

Nathan narrowed his eyes as he absorbed this new piece of the puzzle. "Which means they're surprisingly vulnerable. They're relying on a weapon they barely control."

Jackson considered this. "We can use that overconfidence. If they've neglected their local systems, we might slip through without being detected as long as we keep a low profile and avoid direct confrontation."

Nathan fixed his eyes on the compound. "And go where?"

Jackson frowned but said nothing. Getting in undetected was one thing, but then what? Surrounded by the cold silence of the trees and the ominous presence of the compound, they needed to rethink their plan.

Iris studied the intercepted data on Claire's screen and furrowed her brow as she traced her finger over a set of documents labeled with university names, donors, research funding details, and faculty hiring trends. "This part of the Horsemen's strategy still intrigues me," she murmured. "They're focusing on colleges, research grants, and even academic partnerships. But why?"

Crane's eyes lit up with insight. "It's actually brilliant. Colleges are full of ambitious but impressionable people—idealists—young researchers hungry to, at best, make a difference or, more likely, prove themselves. If the Horsemen can gain a foothold, they can shape these minds to sympathize with their goals, subtly influencing future leaders and intellectuals."

Nathan nodded, his expression grim. "It's like a recruitment drive, but smarter. They don't need to directly convince these people to join them. They train educators with their embedded agenda—like seeds that are cross-pollinated through our public-school systems—encouraging certain narratives and guiding research to benefit their agenda."

Jackson's face hardened as he considered the scope of the plan. "They're creating a generation of unwitting sympathizers. It's...insidious."

Arjun, ever the skeptic, leaned in to peer at the academic documents. "From what I'm seeing, they're pulling it off on a spectacular scale. Funding research, establishing think tanks, embedding people in advisory roles—it's all here."

Iris pondered the implications. "It's terrifying—molding people without their knowledge. It's so subtle, yet so powerful."

Jackson nodded grimly. "Makes you wonder how many of us are influenced without realizing it. The Horsemen know that brute force only gets you so far. But influencing hearts and minds has a lasting effect."

Iris shivered. This wasn't just a power grab. It was a methodical reshaping of society's beliefs and values, preparing fertile ground for the Horsemen's control.

After digesting the disturbing information, the group lingered in the shadowy woods, rethinking their strategy. Jackson stood beside Iris and watched as Nathan and Grice discussed the entry points, their figures dark against the snowy trees.

Grice pulled up schematics for the compound on his tablet. He pointed to a back entrance highlighted on the map, which Arjun had identified as a potential weak spot. "This is our way in," Grice murmured. "The guards' rotations give us a narrow window—maybe five minutes. Once we're inside, we head toward the network hub Arjun pinpointed."

Jackson was frowning but remained silent.

Iris voiced her concerns. "And then what?" She had their attention, but no one responded. They kept circling back to the same issue.

Iris shook her head. "Let's say we get past the guards, they don't notice our footprints in the snow, and we wander the halls undetected—which, let's be honest, seems highly unlikely—what then? We can't just roam around looking through closets and cupboards until we find the Seal."

"No, but we could gather information that might lead us to it," Grice replied sharply.

"And how do we do that?" Iris asked with a wry smile.

A vacant look passed over Grice's face. "I don't know. Hack into their system?"

Iris frowned. "But couldn't we—"

Arjun finished her sentence. "Do that from the outside?"

Claire was already nodding. "Yes."

Nathan exhaled, relieved. "It was good to come here and get the lay of the land."

Jackson looked troubled. "But look at us. We're not exactly Seal Team Six trained to raid a compound."

"True. And hacking into their system is certainly helpful..." Iris replied.

Jackson narrowed his eyes. "But...?"

She shrugged. "But that won't be enough. At some point, we've got to get our hands on that Seal."

Nathan, who'd been listening thoughtfully, added, "And dismantle their whole operation."

Grice rolled his eyes. "We knew all that before."

Crane shot an unreadable look at Grice, then turned to the others. "This isn't a linear issue, so let's stop thinking that way." When met with blank stares, he continued, "Coming here has given us vital information, as have the tech insights Arjun and Claire have provided. But it's going to take more than mapping the compound layout and hacking computers. What we can do with that information depends on the people involved. We need to understand who's connected—the power structure, their contacts, areas of expertise, strengths, and weaknesses—everything about them."

Nathan smirked. "Groups like that don't exactly draw up flow charts and take meeting minutes."

Arjun looked up from his laptop. "Look, I get what you're saying. Tech isn't the only answer. There are a lot of moving parts and all that. So how do we get the lion's share of the information we need?"

Silence hung in the air for several seconds, then Iris said softly, "Go into the lion's den."

Before she could elaborate, Jackson said, "But I thought we decided we weren't going to storm the Bastille."

Iris smiled. "We don't have to. If they're focusing their efforts on the academic world, then an academic who happens to have worked closely with Margaret might be invited into the compound without raising suspicion."

"No," Jackson said flatly.

Iris couldn't believe he'd shot down her idea without hearing her out, so she patiently said, "Yes." Before Jackson could protest again, she went on. "She knows we're aware of the Seal."

"All the more reason for her to doubt your motives," Jackson exclaimed.

Nathan studied Jackson for a moment, then turned to Iris. "Go on."

"If I can convince Margaret that I'm aware of the Horsemen and interested in joining…"

Jackson rolled his eyes. "It's not a birthday party. They're not just going to send you an invite."

Iris shot a blank stare. "I could if I convinced Margaret I've got helpful knowledge or maybe even another artifact."

Jackson silently stared at the compound. "Okay. I'll admit it might work."

Iris smiled. *Finally!*

"But I'll do it. I'm an academic. I know Margaret, too. And I'm a professor," Jackson continued.

Iris's jaw dropped. "Are you kidding me? So, you're going to pull rank?"

"I'm just looking for the most likely path to success."

Iris raised her chin. "Which would be me." She looked from Jackson to the others, none of whom appeared eager to jump into the fray. "Because I'm a woman. We confide in each other more easily."

Jackson ran his hand through his hair. "I can't believe what I'm hearing. You think you can girl-talk your way into the compound and locate the Seal?"

Iris glared at him. "I wouldn't put it exactly that way, but…yes."

Jackson's eyes brightened with anger. "I won't let you do it."

With shocked disbelief, Iris said, "Oh, really? You won't let me?"

"W-well, no," Jackson stuttered. His eyes softened, diffusing Iris's anger. He looked down, but it was too late to hide his true feelings. "I can't put you at risk."

"Let me rephrase what I said. I'm going. It's my decision to make," Iris said gently.

Nathan cleared his throat. "Not exactly. We're a team, so we'll decide as a team—back at the cabin."

THE LATE MORNING light filtered softly through the snow-laced trees as the team settled back at their safe house, reviewing their notes and newly gathered intel.

Arjun paused his typing and broke the silence. "Hey, I might've found something."

The others looked over as he turned the screen to show an event flier. "Margaret Verplanck is listed as a speaker at a symposium on 'New Frontiers in Academia and Information.' It's tomorrow evening at SUNY Plattsburgh."

Jackson raised an eyebrow. "That's not far away."

Arjun nodded. "Less than an hour."

"'New Frontiers in Academia and Information.'" Jackson rolled his eyes. "Typical academia. All words, no meaning."

Arjun glanced at Jackson, then read on. "It's part of a broader initiative—academic leaders addressing information integrity in the digital age, that sort of thing. It'd be the perfect platform to advance the Horsemen's goals in an academic setting."

Iris leaned closer, her interest piqued. "I could attend."

Jackson raised an eyebrow. "As could I."

Nathan held up his hand to stop them. "You'll both go. She knows you both, so it wouldn't be out of place for you to be there together."

Crane voiced his approval, and Grice nodded in agreement. Nathan looked at Arjun and Claire. "Any thoughts?"

Claire shrugged. "Sounds fine to me."

"Me, too," added Arjun.

Nathan practically smiled. "Good. Then we'll try that approach."

Jackson looked over at Iris, catching her determination. "Just be aware that knowing us is a double-edged sword. If she suspects anything, she might cut us off with that sword."

Iris reluctantly agreed. "True, but she's ambitious. If we appeal to that—show her we're intrigued by her work and bring something to the table—she could see us as potential allies or resources."

Iris waited for Jackson to respond. He had that deep-in-thought look he always got when something was troubling him. When she couldn't wait any longer, Iris sighed impatiently. "What?"

"Oh, nothing. I was just wondering what we actually bring to the table."

Iris tried to ignore the knowing look Jackson cast her way. "Nothing, really. But she doesn't need to know that. In the meantime, we'll come up with something."

Jackson winced but said nothing.

After some discussion, the team agreed on the plan. They spent the rest of the day preparing Iris and Jackson for the symposium, drafting questions that would subtly encourage Margaret's interest without revealing their intentions. Arjun worked with Claire on the technical side, making sure their monitoring systems were ready to go in case they needed to intervene.

IRIS FINALLY GAVE up trying to sleep. Wrapping herself in a throw blanket, she went to the window and stared out at the full moon's light and the dark shadows it cast on the snow. When the floor creaked behind her, she turned to find Jackson with his hair in even more disarray than usual.

"Couldn't sleep either?" she asked.

Jackson shook his head. "Look, I'm sorry."

While a reflexive *For what?* came to mind, Iris resisted the impulse to say it because she knew the answer. Instead, she chose to wait.

"I know I came off as some sort of Neanderthal jerk."

He looked so contrite Iris almost forgave him right there. Instead, she suppressed a smirk. "I wouldn't say Neanderthal. Cro-Magnon, maybe."

Jackson shut his eyes for a moment. "So I was a jerk. But in my defense, it was never a male/female power thing." He exhaled. "It was a me/you thing."

With that, he lost any ground he'd gained with Iris, and now her annoyance was mounting. "You mean a me/you power thing?"

"No! A me/you...love thing." Jackson looked nearly as surprised as she was.

Iris couldn't find the means to react. She was frozen except for her heart, which was wildly beating.

Jackson began to backpedal. "Wow. That was...a little abrupt. I didn't mean to say that so soon." he added under his breath, "Or out loud." When he finally made eye contact with her, he said, "Look, forget what I said."

"Forget it?" That was not going to happen, especially after she gave in to an impulse, took hold of his face, and kissed him. It was short. The next instant, they pulled away, staring. All Iris could think was, *What have I done?*

"Well, there you have it," Jackson said softly with a helpless shrug. He leaned closer and touched his lips gently to hers, and they kissed in the moonlight. When it ended, he wrapped his arms around Iris and held her. "I didn't want you to go because I didn't want anything to happen to you."

"That works both ways, you know."

Jackson looked a bit sheepish. "Yeah, I guess."

"So, we'll look out for each other. That's all."

With a nod, Jackson drew Iris back into his arms and held her until it felt as though nothing could harm them.

TWELVE

The next evening, a hum of anticipation buzzed in the air as Iris and Jackson entered the lecture hall along with the other attendees. A banner by the podium prominently displayed Margaret's name.

Iris and Jackson took seats near the back, where they kept a low profile while waiting. Soon, Margaret took the podium, her presence commanding the room. Dressed in a sleek power suit, she exuded authority. Her gaze was steady as she began to speak in a smooth, practiced voice.

"Good evening, everyone. Tonight, I'm honored to discuss an issue at the heart of academia: 'Academic Integrity in the Age of Information Wars.' In a time when data and misinformation are weaponized, it's up to us, educators and researchers, to protect the truth."

Margaret's speech was confident, each word deliberate. She portrayed academia as the last line of defense against misinformation, appealing to the scholarly audience's sense of purpose. However, the underlying message was clear to Iris—control information and you control society.

As applause filled the room, Margaret stepped down to mingle with the attendees. Iris and Jackson waited for the surrounding crowd to thin out before approaching her together.

Margaret's eyes lit up as she recognized them. "Iris! Jackson! I didn't expect to see you here."

"We heard you were speaking and couldn't resist stopping by." Iris smiled, keeping her tone light. "We never got to say a proper goodbye," she added gently.

Margaret's eyes darted nervously away, but she quickly recovered. "Yes. I'm so sorry. I was called away by a family emergency. But everything's fine now." She smiled warmly.

Iris decided to move on. "Your topic is so timely, especially given everything going on in the world."

Jackson nodded. "You made a lot of great points, Margaret. The idea that academia should be the gatekeeper of truth is a powerful concept."

Margaret's face softened, and she nodded approvingly. "It's a challenging time for educators. It's not just about teaching facts—it's about preparing bright young minds for leadership roles to affect change for good in social and public policies."

Iris leaned in slightly. Her expression was earnest. "I'd love to learn more about your current work, Margaret. It sounds like you're taking a very active approach."

Margaret regarded them both thoughtfully and then gave a subtle nod. "Very active. In fact, I think you'd be particularly interested, given your...recent experiences." She gave them a knowing look. "I'm part of a research initiative that is somewhat removed from the traditional academic structure. But we're committed to the same principles—preserving integrity and guiding narratives."

Jackson maintained an intrigued expression. "It sounds like the kind of work we'd be interested in. Academia can feel...limiting at times."

Margaret smiled, pleased by his response. "Exactly."

Iris hesitated, recalling how Margaret's exposure to the Seal had been under duress. "So...what is it you're doing, exactly? Is it something to do with the Seal?" she asked softly.

Margaret glanced around. "I hear it's gone missing."

Iris wasn't sure how to respond. She was certain Margaret had taken the Seal—or at least arranged for its disappearance—but she seemed earnest.

Jackson came to the rescue. "Yes, it's gone, and no one seems to know where it is."

"I see," Margaret said with a slow nod.

"Yes, well...you were telling us about your work."

Margaret's eyes brightened. "We're a selective group. I'd have to get authorization to share any more, but I'll see what I can do. I'll give you a call. And Iris, we should get together sometime to catch up and discuss your career goals. We might have more in common than you realize."

"I'd love that, Margaret," Iris replied.

Another attendee approached Margaret, so Iris and Jackson said their goodbyes and made their way to the exit. With any luck, they had secured a way into the Horsemen's compound.

BACK AT THE SAFE HOUSE, Jackson and Iris laid out the details of their conversation with Margaret for the team while Arjun and Claire unpacked boxes of new equipment.

"She invited us—tentatively—to the compound," Iris explained. "She was vague, but I think she might see us as potential recruits."

Jackson leaned forward. "It's strange, though."

Nathan's eyes narrowed. "How so?"

Jackson thought for a moment. "It's probably nothing. It's just... She seemed a little off her game."

Nathan turned to Iris with a questioning look, but she shrugged. "She'd just given a speech. She was probably tired."

Jackson didn't disagree, but he still looked troubled.

"Anyway, the important thing is that we've practically got an invite to the compound," Iris said.

"No doubt aided by our knowledge of the Seal."

Iris nodded. "Well, yes. We bring something to the table—or at least we appear to."

"Still, she might be ready to bring us into the fold, but she still has to convince the rest of her team," Jackson added.

Nathan looked resolute. "We'd best prepare now. Once you get the green light, we won't have much time. So, let's assume for now that you're going. Once you're in, stay alert. Margaret knows both of you well, and if she senses anything off, she could turn on you. Arjun, Claire, set up some discrete coms and monitor any shifts in their conversations, security—anything that gives you the slightest inkling of concern."

Arjun nodded, setting up his equipment. "I'll keep tabs on the compound's network and be ready to alert them if there's a change. Claire and I will keep you linked in case we need to coordinate an exit."

Nathan looked Jackson in the eye. "Be careful." He turned to Iris. "Trust your gut. If something doesn't feel right, get out. We can try again later."

But Iris knew that another attempt would be nearly impossible. Nathan had to know that, as well. She met Jackson's gaze and, ignoring the nerves in the pit of her stomach, steeled herself and gave him a confident nod.

As midnight approached, Iris sat at the cabin's small kitchen table, poring over Margaret's symposium speech notes that Claire had managed to hack from the university's system. The cabin was quiet except for the soft clicking of keyboards. Claire and Arjun were still working. Their faces were illuminated by the blue glow of their screens. Jackson dozed on the couch. His breathing was steady and deep.

Iris had been tracking changes in Margaret's academic writing over the past year, looking for shifts in her ideology. However, something else captured her attention—a pattern in the terminology that felt too precise to be accidental.

"Claire," Iris called softly, not wanting to wake Jackson. "Can you pull up Margaret's previous speeches? The ones from the last six months?"

Claire nodded. Her fingers drummed on the keyboard. "Already downloaded them. Here."

Iris began highlighting specific phrases across multiple speeches. "Look at this progression. Six months ago, she was using standard academic language. But then there's this shift. She starts incorporating quantum mechanics terminology—as metaphors at first, but then in specific contexts." Iris pointed to several examples. "Quantum leaps in understanding, parallel paths of knowledge, collapsing wave functions of information."

Arjun leaned over, studying the pattern. "That is odd for a historian, especially considering what I found earlier." He pulled up another window. "I've been tracking the Horsemen's shell companies and following the money trails. They've been purchasing industrial-grade quantum computing components. Not just a few but enough to build something massive."

Claire typed at lightning speed. "Cross-referencing

with their power consumption... The energy readings from their compound are off the charts, far more than what cryptocurrency mining would require. And look at these electromagnetic signatures."

"What kind of emissions?" Jackson asked, now awake and joining them.

"That's the strange part," Claire said, frowning at her screen. "It's unlike anything I've seen before. Some kind of directed energy pattern that doesn't match any known frequency."

"I might be able to explain that," Grice said from the doorway, making them all jump. He stepped into the kitchen, looking exhausted. "I've spent months building profiles on every known member of the Horsemen—backgrounds, skills, and patterns. However, about six months ago, something changed. Medical records started showing up—hospitalizations, specialists' consultations, all heavily encrypted."

He pulled out his phone, showing them the documents he'd collected. "It took time to piece it together, but they're all showing similar symptoms—vestibular disruption, neurological damage, and unexplained tissue trauma. At first, I thought they'd been exposed to some kind of microwave weapon, but..." He glanced at Nathan. "It's the Seal, isn't it?"

Nathan emerged from the shadows. His expression was grim. "You found it."

"Found what?" Jackson asked, moving closer to Iris.

"The missing piece—the reason the Horsemen are rushing their timeline," Nathan explained. "The Seal isn't just powerful. It's dangerous. Like a directed energy weapon without proper containment. The more they use it, the more it affects them."

Grice nodded, pulling up more files. "The electromagnetic signatures match the timeframe when they first acquired the Seal. But here's where it gets interesting—the effects aren't consistent. Some members are deteriorating faster than others. And then there's this." He displayed a heavily redacted medical file. "Subject M has been exhibiting similar symptoms but at a much slower rate."

"Margaret," Iris breathed, realizing the connection. "That's why she seems so...off."

Claire was already diving deeper into the encrypted files. "Wait—there's more. Another set of medical records linked to Margaret's file but with different markers. Subject M junior..." Her voice trailed off as she worked to decrypt the data.

"The encryption is complex," Arjun noted, joining her efforts. "Military-grade but with some unusual modifications." They worked together, their fingers flying over their keyboards in synchronized determination.

"Got it," Claire announced after several tense minutes. "Emma Verplanck, age nineteen. Margaret's daughter."

"Emma?" Iris interrupted. "But she's at college somewhere." She shot a questioning look at Jackson, but he shook his head.

Claire scanned through the decrypted files, her

expression growing more troubled. "No, she's being held in a specialized containment unit because she witnessed..." Claire stopped, rereading the text as if to confirm what she was seeing.

"Witnessed what?" Jackson prompted.

"A temporal anomaly," Claire said slowly.

A tense silence fell as they tried to imagine what sort of temporal anomaly could lead the Horsemen to lock Emma up.

"The report describes it as a 'rupture in the space-time continuum.' The electromagnetic readings are off the charts whenever these events occur," Claire continued.

Nathan moved to the window, his posture tense. "The Headless Horseman."

"But that's just a legend," Arjun protested.

"Maybe," Grice said, pulling up another file. "But look at this pattern. Every recorded appearance of the Horseman coincides with massive electromagnetic disturbances. The same kind we're seeing now. It's like the directed energy emissions are somehow...destabilizing local space-time."

A sudden gust of wind rattled the cabin windows, and in the distance, they heard the distinct sound of hoofbeats. The team froze, looking at each other in dawning understanding.

"No way!" Arjun's head snapped toward the sound, and he pushed back from his computer. "A temporal anomaly? A rupture in the space-time continuum? That's friggin' time travel!"

"So the Headless Horseman isn't a ghost," Grice continued, his voice rough. "Based on these readings, it's more like a tear in reality. The electromagnetic fields from the Seal are creating quantum fluctuations. When they spike, moments in time start bleeding through."

"Maybe," Crane interjected.

Iris held up her hand. "Hold on. I need a minute." She looked at Jackson, who appeared equally stunned as he nodded in agreement. Iris began to reason through the situation out loud as the full implications hit her. "Let me get this right. The Seal's electromagnetic emissions are creating these temporal anomalies, and the Horsemen think they can merge it with quantum computing..."

Claire jumped in. "So they can control the time distortions better. They're relying on advanced technology to stabilize its effects."

"But what if they're wrong?" Nathan asked. "What if the Horseman isn't just a random occurrence—it's a warning? Every time someone has tried to push the Seal's power too far, the Horseman has appeared."

As the hoofbeats grew louder, they all moved to the window. Through the moonlit trees, Iris saw it—the Headless Horseman galloping through the snow. But this time, she noticed something else. The air around the figure seemed to ripple and shift like heat waves rising from hot pavement. Through those distortions, she caught impossible glimpses—Continental soldiers marching, vintage cars passing, and scenes from different times bleeding together.

"Claire," Jackson said urgently, "when are they planning to activate their quantum system?"

Claire checked the data. "These power calculations...they're building toward something big." She looked up. "Three days from now."

"Then that's our deadline," Iris said, turning from the window as the Horseman vanished into the night. "We have three days to rescue Margaret's daughter and stop them before they tear reality apart." She shuddered at the gravity of her words.

The weight of their task settled over the room. They weren't just fighting for democracy anymore. They were fighting for the very fabric of reality itself. And somewhere in the Horsemen's compound, a young woman was being held captive, watching as time itself began to fracture around her.

Jackson met Iris's gaze, and in his eyes, she saw the same resolve she felt. Whatever the Horsemen were planning, it had to be stopped. The alternative was unthinkable.

THIRTEEN

Dawn glided over the mountains, painting the snow-covered landscape in shades of silver and blue. Inside the cabin, no one had slept. Empty coffee mugs littered the kitchen counter and sink, and at the table nearby, Claire and Arjun hunched over their laptops and analyzed the data they'd uncovered. At the window, Jackson stood watching the sunrise while Iris organized their findings on a makeshift evidence board she'd created on the cabin wall.

"Three days," Jackson muttered, his breath fogging the cold window. "It's happening then, but we still don't know what they're planning."

Iris stepped back from her wall of notes and photos and rubbed her tired eyes. "We know they're trying to merge quantum computing with the Seal's power, and we know why."

"The question is, why then?" Jackson added.

"More importantly, what then?" Arjun glanced up

from his laptop, then resumed typing. "They must know it's dangerous."

"Maybe they don't have a choice anymore," Claire said, her eyes still fixed on her screen. "These medical records show that all the Horsemen who've had prolonged exposure to the Seal's electromagnetic emissions are experiencing rapid deterioration—dizziness, headaches, visual problems, memory loss, trouble concentrating... Well, you get the idea. It's not good."

Iris's stomach tightened as she shot a quick look at Jackson. "What about us? We've been exposed to the Seal."

Claire looked up, her expression softening. "The directed energy emissions we encountered before were minimal. But now that they're combining it with quantum computing, the power levels are unprecedented."

Crane held up a hand. "Hold on. Plain English. Are you saying the Seal has always given off electromagnetic energy, but now it's gotten worse?"

"Yes, but a minimal amount on its own." Arjun turned his laptop to show them a graph. "Think of it like this. Before, the Seal was potentially dangerous but manageable—like a match. But combine it with quantum computing, and you're lighting that match in the middle of a forest. Which explains why the energy readings from the compound are off the charts."

"And that's what's causing these...tears in time?" Crane asked.

Claire nodded. "Exactly. It's gone way beyond

radio waves. Think of quantum computing as an amplifier. Add that to the Seal, and it's powerful enough to affect the fabric of reality itself."

Arjun pushed back from his laptop and exhaled. "It's like the Havana Syndrome on steroids. The electromagnetic emissions are just the beginning. When combined with quantum computing, they're creating quantum-level disruptions in space-time. And from what I can tell, the system they're building isn't just powerful, it's specific. The components they've acquired are quantum processors, specialized cooling systems, and containment units. If I wanted to stabilize and control the Seal's energy output, that's where I'd start."

"And if they succeed?" Jackson turned from the window.

Nathan leaned on the fireplace mantel. "Could they...control the temporal fractures instead of just causing them—use them deliberately?"

Arjun's eyebrows drew together. "In theory, but—"

A sharp crack echoed through the cabin, making everyone jump. Outside, a strange distortion rippled through the air like a desert mirage. Through the wavering reality, they caught glimpses of something impossible—a Continental Army patrol moved through the trees with crisp new uniforms and muskets at the ready. The soldiers moved with purpose, their boots crunching through the snow.

"Dear God," Crane whispered, leaning against the

window. "Those are Howard's men—Third Regiment. Look at the insignia. I've spent my life studying them, but to see them like this..."

Iris clutched Jackson's arm. "They're so young," she breathed. The soldiers couldn't have been more than boys—their faces fresh and untouched by the war that lay ahead of them.

Claire grabbed a thermal camera and rushed to the window. "Those aren't just images. They've got heat signatures."

"They're real," Arjun said, his voice shaking slightly. "For a moment, they're actually here."

Nathan moved closer to the window, his expression haunted. "I've seen a lot of strange things in my time with the Wardens, but this..." He trailed off as one of the young soldiers turned, seeming to look directly at them. For a heartbeat, past and present met through that impossible gaze.

Then, as quickly as it appeared, the vision faded, leaving them staring at empty, snow-covered trees. The only sound was their collective breathing and Arjun's frantic typing.

"The fractures are getting worse," Grice observed, his usual smugness replaced by genuine concern. "More frequent, more stable. And if that's happening here..."

"We need to understand exactly what we're up against," Iris said, studying her evidence board. "In terms a historian can understand."

Claire smiled faintly and turned her laptop around. "Okay, let me break this down. These are the schematics we found for their quantum computing setup." She pointed to a complex diagram on her screen. "Think of it like a giant magnifying glass for the Seal's power. Regular computers can only perform one calculation at a time, but quantum computers can explore multiple possibilities simultaneously."

"And that matters because...?" Jackson prompted.

"Because the Seal affects reality in ways we don't fully understand," Arjun explained, pulling up another diagram. "These power readings from the compound spike every time there's a temporal anomaly. It's like they're running tests to see how much the quantum system can amplify the effects of the Seal."

Iris moved closer and focused not on the technical diagrams but on the graph showing energy spikes. "So, each of these peaks represents a moment when time... fractures?"

"Exactly," Claire said. "And they're getting higher each time."

A sound from outside drew their attention—hoofbeats growing closer. Jackson moved to the window, and Iris joined him. Through the early morning mist, they saw the Headless Horseman atop his black steed, moving with impossible grace through the trees. But this time, something was different.

"Look at the air around it," Iris whispered, pressing closer to the glass. The space around the Horseman seemed to shimmer and split, showing glimpses of other times—a gleaming 1957 Chevy Bel Air cruising down a dirt road, Revolutionary War soldiers marching in formation, a Model T Ford puttering along where the cabin's driveway would one day be. Each vision layered over the others like old photographs bleeding together.

"It's not just a warning anymore," Nathan said grimly. "It's as if the temporal barriers are breaking down. Past, present, and future are starting to meld together."

As if to confirm his words, the Horseman suddenly multiplied—three identical figures riding in perfect sync through different layers of time, visible through the fracturing reality. Then, as suddenly as they appeared, the visions collapsed into a single rider who vanished into the trees.

Claire's laptop pinged, drawing their attention back inside. "I've decrypted more of Margaret's daughter's medical file," she announced. Her voice was tight. "Emma wasn't just a witness to these anomalies. According to these notes, she has some kind of...electromagnetic hypersensitivity that allows her to detect quantum fluctuations. She can sense when the barriers between time streams are about to rupture."

"That's why they're keeping her," Iris realized. "They're using her to monitor the temporal effects of their experiments."

Jackson's jaw tightened. "Like a canary in a coal mine."

"And we all know what happens to those canaries," Grice added darkly.

"Not necessarily," Arjun said as he studied the data. "The electromagnetic fields in her containment unit mirror the quantum signatures we're seeing from these temporal fractures, but they're carefully controlled. They're using her sensitivity to calibrate their equipment."

"Which means they're learning," Grice added. "Every test, every fracture—they're gathering data to figure out how to harness these effects."

Iris moved back to her evidence board and added new notes with quick, decisive strokes. "So, let's put it all together. The Horsemen have the Seal. They're building a quantum computing system to try to control its power, but that's affecting their health. They're holding Margaret's daughter because she can sense temporal anomalies. And they're planning something here." She pointed to a calendar. "Oh. There's a full moon."

"A full moon?" Claire muttered, typing rapidly. "Think about it—during a full moon, the moon's gravitational pull on the earth is at its strongest. In quantum mechanics, gravity can affect quantum states. So, during a full moon, they could push the Seal to its maximum..." she trailed off, her fingers frozen above her keyboard.

"You lost me," Crane said. "What does gravity have to do with it?"

Arjun leaned forward. "The Seal already creates distortions in space-time, right? And quantum computing works by manipulating quantum states that exist in multiple positions simultaneously. So the moon's gravitational alignment could act like a lens, focusing and amplifying both effects."

"Like a magnifying glass focusing sunlight and starting a fire?" Iris asked.

"Exactly," Claire said. "But instead of focusing light, it's focusing gravitational forces that could enhance both the quantum computing system and the Seal's temporal effects. The calculations I'm seeing... I mean, it's all theoretical at this point, but if they try this during the full moon—and it works—they might be able to control the temporal fractures, or—" She winced.

"More likely, they could lose control and shatter the barriers between time streams completely," Arjun continued.

"And once those barriers break..." Nathan's voice was grim.

"Reality as we know it could collapse," Claire finished.

A heavy silence descended upon the room as the implications of the situation became apparent. Outside, another temporal ripple passed through the landscape, briefly showing the cabin as it had looked two centuries ago, then as it might appear decades in the future, before settling back into the present.

"So, what's our next move?" Jackson asked, his hand finding Iris's without thinking.

Nathan stood, his expression resolute. "We split up. One team goes after Emma—not just to save her but to deprive them of their temporal early warning system.

The other team infiltrates the compound to gather intel on their quantum computing setup. We need to know exactly what we're trying to stop."

"I'll take point on the rescue," Grice offered. "I know their security systems and their patrol patterns."

"I'll go with you," Arjun said. "They'll be using tech to monitor Emma. We'll need to bypass it."

Claire looked up from her laptop. "I should go too. Those temporal readings... If Emma really can sense the anomalies, we might need that ability."

"Then Jackson and I will handle the lab infiltration," Iris said. "We already have our cover story from the symposium. Margaret knows us, trusts us—at least partly."

"Or she'll see through you immediately," Nathan warned. "Be careful."

Another temporal ripple washed over the landscape outside, stronger than before. Through the windows, they watched as reality flickered between past, present, and possible futures, each shift accompanied by a strange sound and vibrating pressure in their ears.

"Three days," Jackson said, squeezing Iris's hand. "Let's make them count."

Jackson's phone buzzed. The screen flickered with static before displaying a text from Margaret.

Tomorrow morning. 10 am. Let's discuss your ideas about academic integrity. Meet me at the gate at the end of the old fire road on Lyon Mountain.

Jackson stared at the phone, then typed a quick,

professional response. When he looked up, his face was grim. "Well, we wanted a way in. Now we have it."

"And a deadline," Iris added. She turned to the board and added one final note. Among her theories and connections, a single question stood out. "What happens when time itself breaks?" She didn't want to find out.

FOURTEEN

The Adirondack Mountains loomed ahead. Their snow-covered peaks were shrouded in low clouds as Jackson maneuvered the truck up a treacherously winding mountain road. Next to him, Iris double-checked the old blueprints that Claire had discovered.

Jackson glanced over at her. "I wouldn't count on that being the same."

After shooting him a look of mild annoyance, Iris said, "Really? Because I was hoping to score a set of Cold War-era bucket chairs for my apartment. What do you think—avocado or orange?"

Jackson suppressed a grin. "Sorry. I didn't mean to be..."

"Condescending?"

He winced. "Well...yeah, I guess that sums it up."

Iris smiled. "I was actually trying to imagine if I were a Horseman, how would I make use of this space? It makes the most sense to set up shop in the tall radar tower for starters, then expand to the others over time. Of course, it would depend on their condition. If the structures are sound, they've probably configured the inside with living quarters and at least one security room—probably toward the top. Don't you think? That's where I'd start looking for Emma."

Jackson nodded, but his eyes remained fixed on the road. "There's only one road in and out, so we could find ourselves cornered. In that case, the only way out is on foot."

A grouping of towers appeared at the top of the mountain. Corrugated metal and cement jutted up from the ground, surrounded by tall fencing.

"There's the security gate," Jackson muttered as they approached a checkpoint that looked more military than academic.

A guard stepped out of the booth, a handgun clearly visible beneath his heavy coat.

Jackson tightened his grip on the wheel and stopped the truck. He reminded himself that they'd rehearsed this. They were ready.

The guard checked their IDs with professional efficiency before making a call. After a moment, he nodded. "Dr. Verplanck will meet you at the main entrance."

As THEY PULLED into the parking area, Iris caught her first glimpse of Margaret as she stepped outside to greet them. They grabbed their briefcases and hurried through the bitter cold to the entrance, where a welcome blast of warm air met them.

Margaret's smile was strained as she approached. "Jackson, Iris—thank you for coming." Her voice wavered slightly, and dark circles shadowed her eyes.

"The drive wasn't too difficult?" Margaret asked, her tone oddly formal.

"Not at all," Jackson assured her. "The directions were perfect."

Margaret nodded. "Good. Well, why don't I show you around?"

Before Jackson could respond, a voice called from across the lobby, "Jackson Wilde! Don't tell me you finally got tired of the classroom!"

They turned to see a tall woman striding toward them, her silver hair gleaming in the winter sunlight that streamed in through the windows. Dr. Eleanor Thorne moved with confidence. Her smile was warm, but her eyes were sharp as she evaluated them.

"Eleanor," Jackson said, genuine warmth in his voice. "What a pleasant surprise."

Thorne embraced him briefly before stepping back to study him. "Can you believe it's been three years since that curriculum committee? I still say you were too soft on the classical requirements."

Iris felt an unexpected twinge of...something. Jealousy? The easy familiarity between Jackson and this elegant, accomplished woman made her feel suddenly young and out of her depth.

"Yes, but we put it to a vote—the democratic process in action," Jackson replied, his tone light but pointed.

"Always the idealist," Thorne said with a smile, then turned to Iris. "And this must be Dr. Drake. Margaret's told me so much about your work on Revolutionary War-era grassroots movements."

"Dr. Thorne," Iris acknowledged, keeping her voice professionally neutral. "It's so nice to meet you."

Thorne smiled, but it didn't reach her eyes. "How do you like our little facility? It's a work in progress, but we're very excited about it. Margaret, why don't we give them the tour? Show them what real academic freedom looks like."

"Yes, of course. We should start with—" Margaret said.

"The research wing," Thorne interrupted as she wedged herself between Jackson and Iris. "I insist. You'll be fascinated by our approach to information integrity, Jackson. It's quite different from those endless faculty senate debates."

As they followed Thorne through the security checkpoint and up a winding flight of stairs, Iris noticed how the workplace environment changed. The comfortable academic facade of the ground floor was gone, replaced by stark white walls and harsh, clinical lighting. Their footsteps echoed on the tile floors.

"We've organized our research into specialized units," Thorne explained as they walked. "Each team focuses on a specific aspect of information control—that is, integrity."

Jackson and Iris exchanged a glance at the slip, but Thorne continued as if nothing had happened. She led them past laboratories where researchers hunched over complex equipment.

"The integration of quantum computing has opened up possibilities we never imagined," Thorne said as they approached an intersection of hallways. "We're not just studying history anymore. We're improving it. Or we will be, once—"

She stopped abruptly as they neared a restricted corridor. Through the reinforced windows, Iris saw what looked like containment cells. For just a moment, she thought she saw a young woman pressed against the glass, her terrified face familiar from the medical files. *Emma?*

"This way," Thorne said sharply, her warm demeanor cracking slightly. "The demonstration theater is just ahead. I think you'll find it quite illuminating."

They entered what appeared to be a medical theater with tiered seating surrounding a central demonstration area. However, instead of surgical equipment, the room was filled with an array of quantum computing machinery. In the center of it all was an imposing cabinet.

Two researchers rushed to a panel containing a keypad and entered a long sequence of codes. The panel split diagonally to reveal a hidden chamber bathed in an otherworldly blue glow. In it, suspended and rotating in a cylinder of light, was the Seal. Iris found Jackson's hand.

The Seal looked both ancient, with its weathered bronze surface catching the light, yet impossibly new as it shimmered and turned to highlight strange symbols along its edge. The quantum computing equipment surrounded it like a technological altar, sleek modern machinery humming with barely contained power.

As stunning as the sight was, it was the feeling that struck Iris the hardest—a sense of heaviness in the air that had nothing to do with the Seal's physical form. It was an object that had witnessed the birth of a nation.

"My God," Jackson whispered.

Even Margaret, who must have seen it countless times, seemed transfixed.

Thorne watched them with proud light in her eyes. "Margaret told me you've already had a preview of what the Seal is capable of, so you can imagine why we need such precise containment."

The Seal pulsed, sending a wave of temporal energy through the room while a piercing blue radiance seemed to fill the surrounding space. Iris tightened her grip on Jackson's hand as the air shimmered around them.

"Impressive, isn't it?" Thorne said, noting their reactions. "The marriage of past and future. The Founders could never have imagined how we would perfect their vision."

Thorne moved to an instrument panel, her fingers

dancing across the controls with practiced ease. "The quantum system allows us to direct the Seal's energy with electromagnetic pulses—to control it rather than merely contain it. Would you like a demonstration?"

Before they could respond, the Seal began to pulse with an otherworldly light. Iris flinched.

"Not to worry," Thorne said, smiling. "The quantum containment field is completely stable."

Despite her assurances, Thorne kept glancing at a readout on her screen. "We've learned from our early... miscalculations."

A technician's face turned ashen as he adjusted some settings. "Dr. Thorne, wait. The quantum error correction isn't stable at these power levels."

"Nonsense!" Thorne's voice was sharp. "Our guests need to understand what we're accomplishing." She turned to Jackson. "We're about to change everything. Imagine a world of pure, perfect order. No more of democracy's inefficiencies. No more protests, demonstrations, or chaos."

The humming grew louder, and the air itself seemed to vibrate with potential energy. Warning lights began to flash on the control panel, and an alarm sounded.

Jackson's ears began ringing with painful intensity. "Eleanor, something's wrong!"

The Seal's pulsing became erratic, and reality rippled like a heat mirage. Jackson reached for Iris, but it was too late.

The world fractured.

ONE MOMENT, Iris was standing in the theater. The next, she was in a forest. This wasn't the gentle snowfall of moments ago. The air was thick with gun smoke, and the crack of musket fire split the air.

Men in Colonial militia uniforms crashed through the underbrush, pursued by red-coated British soldiers. They ran right through Iris as if she were a ghost—or perhaps they were the ghosts.

A musket ball splintered the tree beside her head.

Ghost or not, that felt real enough.

The battlefield materialized around her with shocking clarity—not like watching a movie or reading a book, but with all the sensory assault of reality. The acrid smell of gunpowder burned her nostrils. Her winter clothing felt hot in the eighteenth-century summer.

A young militiaman staggered past, clutching his shoulder, where blood seeped between his fingers. He couldn't have been more than sixteen, his eyes wide with terror and pain. Without thinking, Iris reached for him, but her hand passed through his arm like smoke.

"Fall back!" The cry came from somewhere ahead. "To the fort! Fall back!"

The soldiers seemed to run through her, yet the ground beneath her feet felt solid and real enough. The historian in her noticed details her mind struggled to process—their weapons—muskets, long rifles, and pistols—the mix of proper uniforms and homespun clothing.

An officer on horseback galloped past, shouting orders through the chaos. "Hold the line! We can't lose the fort!"

The tactical implications struck her. This had to be during Burgoyne's campaign when the British were trying to cut off New England from the other colonies.

More musket fire erupted. The sound was nothing like what she'd heard in movies or reenactments—it was sharp and reverberated through her bones. Not ten feet away, a British soldier emerged from the smoke, his red coat vivid against the green foliage. He raised his musket, aiming at a colonial militia member who had stumbled. Without thinking, Iris shouted a warning.

The British soldier's head snapped toward her. For a heart-stopping moment, their eyes met. His widened in shock. He could see her. The impossible connection lasted only a second before another volley of gunfire sent him diving for cover.

The smoke thickened, and the sounds of battle pressed in from all sides. One minute, Iris felt pressure on her head, and the next, she felt dizzy and disconnected. Was she becoming more solid in this time or fading away completely? Would she disappear like smoke if she couldn't get back?

A cannon boomed from the fort's walls, and then, the world seemed to flicker. For a moment, she saw the modern demonstration theater overlaid against the forest, like a double exposure in an old photograph. In the distance, she heard Jackson's voice, distorted as if underwater. He was calling her name.

Then reality snapped back to the past, and the battle pressed in closer. Iris dove behind a fallen log as more shots rang out. Through the smoke and chaos, she saw Fort Ticonderoga in the distance, its walls solid and new. She was trapped in 1777. With each passing second, the world she knew was slipping further away.

And somewhere, she heard Jackson screaming her name.

FIFTEEN

One moment, she was there, solid and real, her hand almost touching his. The next, she faded into the mist, her eyes wide with fear as she reached for Jackson. He lunged forward, but his fingers passed through the empty space where she'd been, grasping nothing but air. The area where Iris had stood felt warmer with a quantum distortion that made his skin crawl.

"Iris!" he cried out desperately, his voice echoing off the theater's curved walls. Around him, the observation room erupted into barely controlled chaos. Warning lights flashed while technicians scrambled between their stations. The quantum computing equipment that had seemed so impressive moments ago now hummed with a frequency that set Jackson's teeth on edge.

Through the reinforced window, the Seal's glow had intensified from a soft phosphorescence to a piercing radiance that seemed to bend the light around it. Jackson's historian's mind—the part that wasn't screaming in panic—absurdly noted that no Revolutionary War artifact should be capable of this. The implications of that thought threatened to overwhelm him, but he forced it aside. Right now, only one thing mattered.

Jackson spun toward Thorne at the control panel. "Bring her back. Now!"

Eleanor Thorne's fingers raced over the keyboard with speed and precision despite the crisis. Jackson searched her face for any trace of the colleague he'd known at Columbia—the woman who'd fought so passionately for academic integrity. Her expression now was almost clinical, despite the emergency klaxons and flashing warnings.

"The temporal displacement shouldn't manifest this way," she muttered, more to herself than to him. "The containment field was supposed to—"

"I don't care what it was supposed to— It didn't!" Jackson slammed his hand on the console, making several technicians jump. The pain in his palm brought him back to reality—a reality that was becoming increasingly unstable. "Get her back!"

A young researcher monitoring the quantum readings spoke up, his voice shaking, "Dr. Thorne, the temporal field is expanding. We're seeing anomalies throughout the facility."

"Contain it," Thorne ordered sharply. "Redirect power from the auxiliary systems if you have to."

Margaret stepped forward, her hands trembling as

she gripped her tablet. Her usual precise demeanor was cracking, revealing her distress.

"Eleanor," she said, her voice carefully controlled, "we need to stabilize the field before—"

"I know what we need to do!" Thorne cut her off with a sharp look that made Margaret fall silent.

There was some history in that look, Jackson realized, along with a warning that made Margaret's knuckles whiten around her tablet.

While Thorne turned back to the controls, Margaret moved closer to Jackson, her voice barely a whisper. "This happened to Emma. She saw something —a temporal anomaly in the library archives. I thought she was having a breakdown when she tried to tell me." Her voice caught. "Then they showed me the security footage. She witnessed a complete temporal shift, just like this. Now they say they need to 'contain' her."

Jackson kept his eyes on Thorne's back, speaking as quietly as Margaret had. "Where? Are they holding her here?"

Margaret gave a slight nod, her face tight with controlled anguish. "That's why I'm here. I've got to find a way to rescue her."

Something didn't make sense. Jackson said, "But if you first thought she was having a breakdown, wouldn't others assume so as well? So why lock her up?"

"All I've been able to glean is that this wasn't the first time. But with Emma, it was different."

"Different? How?"

Margaret's face contorted with worry. "She has

some kind of electromagnetic hypersensitivity that lets her detect quantum fluctuations before they happen. She can sense when reality is about to fracture. That's why they're keeping her—to help calibrate their experiments." Her fingers gripped the tablet so hard that Jackson thought it might crack. "If I don't cooperate, they've made threats."

Jackson was stunned. "Dr. Thorne might have gone off the deep end, but I can't imagine her resorting to violence."

Margaret raised her eyebrows. "Maybe not violence, but Eleanor's focused on using the quantum computing system to push the Seal further. Until she gets what she wants, she won't let Emma go."

"And what's that exactly?"

"I don't know. But it's taking a toll." She cast furtive glances at the techs in the room. "Everyone who's been exposed to the Seal's electromagnetic energy has started showing symptoms—headaches, vertigo, nausea..." She paused, her voice softening. "But for Emma, it's worse. I'm afraid it will kill her."

Jackson put a comforting arm on Margaret's shoulder and was about to speak when Dr. Thorne leaned over the technician's table. "Those containment readings can't be right!"

Before the technician could respond, the air rippled like heat waves off hot pavement. For a split second, reality seemed to fold in on itself.

Through the distortion, Jackson saw Iris—not just her image, but Iris standing on a battlefield with a familiar building in the background. Their eyes met across an impossible divide. He reached for her again, but reality snapped back like a rubber band.

"What did you see?" Thorne demanded, her academic interest overtaking her calm facade. Around them, equipment hummed with urgent intensity.

"She's there—in the past, in the midst of a battle." Jackson moved closer to the control panel, forcing himself to think analytically despite his rising panic. The historian in him couldn't help but notice the details —the uniforms, the terrain. "Fort Ticonderoga," he realized. "It must be the siege—in 1777."

"The specific temporal location doesn't matter," Thorne interrupted, but Jackson noticed her reaction. She flinched slightly at the identification as if he'd confirmed something she'd feared.

"Doesn't it?" He studied her face. "The containment protocols, the quantum stabilizers—you've been preparing for something like this." A sudden realization struck him with horror. "This wasn't just an accident, was it?"

Another temporal ripple pulsed through the room, stronger than before. Equipment sparked, and one of the monitoring stations exploded in a shower of sparks. Through the observation window, they watched as reality seemed to blur. It was like looking through a kaleidoscope of time—Colonial soldiers moving through the same space as modern researchers and something else. Something that shouldn't exist yet.

Jackson caught a glimpse of what looked like future

technology, sleek and strange, before that facet of reality twisted away. In that moment, his blood ran cold as he recognized a symbol—one of the symbols etched into the Seal.

"Eleanor," Margaret said softly as she took a half step forward. "Maybe we should tell him. If he understands what we're trying to prevent—"

"That's enough," Thorne snapped. "Remember what's at stake, Margaret. Think of Emma."

Margaret flinched, and Jackson saw real fear in her eyes. The pieces were starting to come together, but the picture they formed was impossible—or should have been.

The quantum systems whined louder, the pitch rising to something almost human. On the monitors, power readings spiked into red zones. Whatever Thorne was trying didn't seem to be working.

"Your containment is failing," Jackson said, forcing his voice to stay calm despite his rising panic. Anger wouldn't help Iris now. Understanding might. "Whatever you think you're preventing, it won't matter if you tear reality apart trying to get there."

"You don't understand," Thorne muttered, trying another sequence. "We're running out of time. The calculations showed us what's coming if we don't—"

She cut herself off, but Jackson caught it. "What calculations? What's coming?"

Before she could answer, another ripple hit—stronger than any before. Through the observation window, reality fractured like glass. Each shard revealed a different time, a different possibility. Jackson caught glimpses that seared themselves into his mind—Washington D.C. in ruins, martial law declarations, democracy crumbling. But it was the time period that stunned him. The cars and the clothing—they weren't from the past.

"My God," he breathed, reeling from the implications. "You're not just studying time. You're trying to change it."

"We're trying to save it!" Thorne's composure cracked. The lights flickered, casting harsh shadows across her face. "Everything we've done—the Seal, the quantum integration—it's all to prevent—" She stopped, visibly forcing herself back under control. "It doesn't matter. What matters is getting these temporal fluctuations under control."

A new alarm joined the cacophony—this one deeper, more urgent. On the monitors, Jackson could see other temporal anomalies forming throughout the compound. Reality was becoming unstable on a massive scale.

"At least tell me this," he said, controlling his fury. "Your 'containment protocols,' will they protect Iris from the quantum distortions? Or is she being exposed to the same electromagnetic pulses that are affecting all of you?"

Thorne slowly shook her head, but Jackson wasn't buying it. "Look at yourselves—dark, sunken eyes. You all look exhausted and anxious. Is anyone even rational anymore?"

Thorne's silence was answer enough.

Another surge rocked the facility. Through the observation window, they watched in horror as reality seemed to tear—past, present, and possible futures bleeding together like watercolors in the rain. The Seal's housing began to crack. Its otherworldly light pulsed in an erratic rhythm that matched the quantum fluctuations.

"Eleanor," Margaret pleaded, "we have to do something. We can't leave Iris there."

But before anyone could answer, the quantum systems screamed in electronic protest. Reality shuddered. Through the observation window, the Seal's glow became blinding.

And somewhere, lost in the chaos of fractured time, Iris fought for survival in a battle that had ended centuries ago.

A MUSKET BALL missed Iris by inches, embedding itself in the tree trunk beside her head. She pressed herself behind a fallen log. Her heart pounded as the sounds of battle surrounded her—gunfire, shouted orders, and the cries of the wounded. This wasn't history anymore. It was horrifyingly real.

Iris fought to suppress her panic as she caught glimpses of a desperate fight through the gun smoke. She realized that she had landed in the siege of Fort Ticonderoga. The British advance was pushing the colonial forces back toward the fortress walls. Now, she could see individual faces—young men who had no idea their deaths would be recorded in history books. Their fear and courage were preserved in the carefully archived documents she'd studied countless times.

A new sound cut through the chaos—a high-pitched whine that didn't belong in 1777. The air rippled, and against the backdrop of the battlefield, the modern laboratory appeared.

She thought she heard Jackson calling her name. The sound sent a surge of hope coursing through her, but it also revealed something terrifying. With each temporal shift, the glimpses of her own time became fainter.

Then reality snapped back, and another volley of musket fire sent her ducking for cover. It made her head spin—or was that the effect of the quantum distortions?

She had to find a way back, but how? If she strayed from this spot seeking safety, she might lose her connection to her own time. As the battle closed in around her and the temporal ripples grew weaker, she felt herself slipping away from the present and into the chaos of battle.

The world was fracturing, and she was trapped on the wrong side of time.

SIXTEEN

The British advance turned into a full assault. Iris pressed herself against the earth as another volley of musket fire tore through the air above her hiding place. Her temporary shelter behind the fallen log wouldn't last much longer. She could hear officers shouting orders, directing troops to outflank the colonial position—and her own.

Smoke hung thick in the air, mixing with the metallic scent of the blood-stained ground. Every sound seemed magnified—the crack of musket fire, the screams of the wounded, and the clomping of boots on the ground. This wasn't the sanitized history of textbooks. This was war in all its terrible immediacy.

A British soldier appeared through the gun smoke no more than twenty yards away, already reloading his musket. Two more followed. They hadn't spotted her yet, but they would. Iris forced herself to think past the panic. She was a historian. She knew how this battle ended. Under General St. Clair, the Americans would abandon Fort Ticonderoga to Burgoyne's forces in a matter of days, retreating south in what was meant to be a strategic withdrawal. The British victory here would prove hollow. The Colonial forces would do their best to make the road impassable as they retreated, felling trees and destroying bridges. This would slow Burgoyne's advance until his eventual defeat at Saratoga. But that historical knowledge wouldn't help her if she died here, trapped in the wrong century.

Movement to her left caught her eye. The air itself seemed to ripple, but this was no heat mirage. Through the temporal distortion, she glimpsed other times—a Model T rattling down a dirt road, modern tourists snapping photos of the fort, and visions of what might have been the future.

Another volley of musket fire rang out, closer this time. Splinters flew as bullets struck the log she was using for cover. She had to move. Now.

Iris pushed herself up and ran. The British soldiers shouted, their voices rising above the chaos of battle. Boots marched through the brush. Muskets fired. Twenty yards to the temporal distortion. Fifteen. Ten.

A bullet whizzed past her ear. Another kicked up dirt at her feet. She didn't look back—couldn't look back. The rippling curtain of fractured time was right in front of her. Through it, she saw fragments of different eras flickering like frames from an old film— Colonial, Victorian, modern-day, and times she couldn't identify. The laboratory she sought wasn't there, but with British troops closing in, she had no choice. She had to escape.

Iris threw herself forward into the temporal maelstrom.

The world dissolved into chaos. Every sense screamed in protest as reality itself seemed to tear apart around her. Colors flooded her vision. Sounds from a dozen different eras blared in a discordant chorus. Her head ached. She was losing her balance. For a moment, she feared she might dissolve completely.

Then, as suddenly as it began, the chaos settled. Iris found herself on her hands and knees in thick mud, gasping for breath. The air was heavy with the scent of approaching rain, and the sky had darkened to a threatening gray. She was still in the past—a woman in an eighteenth-century dress hurried past with a basket—but this wasn't Fort Ticonderoga.

She knew this place. It was Sleepy Hollow.

Before she could process the implications, she heard the thunder of approaching hooves. The sound seemed to come from everywhere as it echoed through the hollow. The few people on the road scattered and disappeared into doorways and behind shuttered windows.

From the mist, a massive horse emerged, its coat as black as storm clouds. Its rider sat tall in the saddle, exuding a military bearing that was obvious even at a distance. He wore the dark blue coat and tall silver helmet of a Revolutionary-era Hessian soldier.

The Horseman reined in his mount beside Iris and

bent down, extending his hand. Iris hesitated. For one thing, the Hessians fought for the British. So, the fact that he found her—seemingly the only woman on a battlefield—should have given him every reason to believe she was an enemy. But she was in danger, and he offered escape—or at least the appearance of it. There was something in his bearing and his striking sapphire blue eyes that offered protection rather than threat. So, she took a chance and reached for his hand.

In one smooth motion, he pulled her up behind him on the horse. No words were spoken—perhaps none were needed. The great horse wheeled around and broke into a gallop.

The world blurred around them as they rode. Iris caught glimpses of different times again—past, present, future—but they passed through them like a mist. The Horseman seemed to know exactly where he was going, guiding his mount through the chaos of fractured time with impossible skill.

They emerged onto another battlefield—not Ticonderoga this time, but a different engagement. The horse slowed, and Iris felt a surge of temporal energy building. The Horseman helped her dismount and then pointed urgently toward a place where the air had begun to ripple.

That was when she saw it—a cannonball—coming directly at the Horseman. He had to have seen it, but he waited as if seeing her to safety were his sole purpose. Or perhaps he had been here before.

"Wait—" she started to say, but it was too late.

The cannonball struck. Iris caught one last glimpse of the Horseman—his head severed cleanly from his shoulders—before the temporal energy swept her away. In that terrible moment, Iris understood. The Headless Horseman was caught in an unending loop of temporal fractures, doomed to journey through the past and the present without ever arriving at his future.

Reality twisted one final time. The battlefield dissolved into the stark lighting of the laboratory. Iris staggered, and her legs gave way beneath her. She was falling, but strong arms caught her and held her.

"Iris!" Jackson's voice was ragged with relief as he pulled her close.

She buried her face in his chest and breathed in his familiar scent while his solid presence. His heart hammered against her cheek as his arms tensed around her.

"I thought I'd lost you," he whispered into her hair. "When you disappeared..." His voice broke.

She pulled back just enough to look up at him and see both fear and relief in his eyes. Without thinking about the crisis still unfolding around them, she said softly, "I heard you calling through time."

Jackson cupped her face in his hands and kissed her —a kiss that felt like coming home. For just a moment, nothing else mattered—not the Seal, not the temporal anomalies, or the watching eyes of those around her. Just this. Just Jackson.

When she finally looked up, she saw Margaret, Thorne, and the others staring at her. They couldn't know what she'd witnessed or understand the truth she'd discovered about one of history's most enduring legends.

The Headless Horseman wasn't just a ghost story. He was real. Like Iris, he'd been caught in a temporal vortex long enough to understand the forces that shaped history—forces like the Seal. In its midst, he had happened upon Iris and saved her.

Iris looked at the Seal, still glowing in its containment field, and wondered how many other secrets it held. Did others like the Headless Horseman wander through time, confined by unseen boundaries?

The answer, she suspected, was encoded in the Seal itself. If they could only understand it before time unraveled completely.

THE REUNION WAS SHATTERED by a high-pitched whine from the quantum equipment. The Seal's glow had intensified, and Jackson felt a headache coming on from the quantum distortions.

"The temporal barriers are collapsing," Thorne announced, her composed facade cracking as she frantically worked at the controls. "The quantum stabilizers can't contain it."

The air rippled, and for a moment, the laboratory vanished, replaced by a Colonial-era meeting house. Through the windows, Jackson glimpsed other time periods flickering past like channels on an old tube television—horse-drawn carriages sharing the same space as modern cars and people from different centuries walking through each other.

"Eleanor," Margaret said, her voice tight with fear, "shut it down."

"I can't!" Thorne pounded the keys in rapid bursts. "The quantum integration is too deep. If I terminate it now, I don't know what will happen."

Another surge rocked the facility. Emergency sirens blared as reality itself seemed to shudder.

OUTSIDE, Nathan, Crane, and Grice arrived at the tree line, closely followed by Arjun and Claire. They took up a position overlooking the compound. Arjun stared at his laptop screen in disbelief. "These readings can't be right."

Claire leaned in, her eyes widening. "The energy signatures... They're exponential. What's going on in there?"

They watched as guards abandoned their posts and fled the compound. One man crashed into a fence that hadn't existed moments before, then scrambled away as it vanished again.

"We've got to get in there," Claire said, already packing her equipment. "Jackson and Iris don't understand quantum mechanics. If the containment fails completely—"

"Look!" Arjun pointed to where several black

SUVs were peeling out of the compound's parking area. "The Horsemen are fleeing their own compound."

Nathan stepped forward from the shadows. "That's our opening. Grice?"

Grice checked his weapon. "Or maybe they know something we don't."

Nathan shot a harsh look at Grice. "Maybe, but we're going in."

Grice eyed Nathan as if he'd lost his mind. "You can't go in there. They'll recognize you."

"Does it really matter at this point? I'm going. You can join us or not."

"The security systems are probably compromised by the temporal fluctuations. We can use that," Claire said.

"Then let's move," Crane said grimly. "Before there's no reality left to save."

BACK IN THE LABORATORY, Jackson held Iris steady as another wave of quantum distortion washed through the room. The walls appeared to breathe, shifting between modern clinical white and ancient stone.

"The Seal," Iris gasped. "What's it trying to do?"

The artifact's glow had taken on a strange pattern, almost like a heartbeat. Each pulse sent out waves of temporal distortion that grew stronger by the second.

"It's not trying to do anything," Thorne said. Her voice was hollow. "It's trying to undo everything. All our work, all our plans..." She stared numbly at the readings on her screen. "We thought we could control it—direct it. We just wanted to undo history's wrongs so we could avoid future disasters that were based on the past."

The main doors burst open. Arjun and Claire rushed in, followed closely by Nathan, Crane, and Grice. They must have fought their way through the chaos to reach the lab. Their clothes were disheveled, and Crane sported a bloody lip.

"The compound is coming apart," Arjun announced, already moving to study the quantum equipment. "Reality is unraveling at the quantum level."

Claire joined him, her fingers flying over a secondary control panel. "The Seal's quantum entanglement with the system is complete. If we try to disengage them, it could shatter the barriers between time streams."

"Then what do we do?" Jackson demanded.

Claire had no answer.

A moment of relative quiet fell over the lab during a calm between temporal surges briefly stabilized. Nathan took advantage of it and moved to stand beside his son. For a moment, father and son exchanged glances at the pulsing Seal together, both at the mercy of what the artifact would do next.

"All those years I was gone," Nathan said softly, "I told myself I was protecting you—that staying away was the right thing to do." He gripped Jackson's shoulder. "I was wrong. We should have faced our battles together. It's what families do."

Jackson met his father's gaze. After all the years they had lost, it might be too late, but this was their second chance. He tried to smile. "I'm in. But you picked a hell of a place to start."

That moment was abruptly broken by a new sound —a deep thrumming that seemed to emanate from the Seal itself. The artifact's glow intensified until it was almost blinding.

"Oh, crap," Claire breathed, staring at her readings. "It's not merging time periods anymore. They're collapsing. All of them. Into a single point."

The air began to crystallize around them as reality prepared to implode.

SEVENTEEN

A strange quantum distortion flickered at the back of Iris's mind as she clung to Jackson, steadying herself after her harrowing return from the distant battlefield and the inconceivable ride with the Horseman. The bitter tang of burned wiring hung in the thick air of the lab. Overhead alarms screeched, and sparks spat from several fried consoles.

Claire hovered by the quantum console. Conduits coiled around her arms like serpents as she frantically reconnected them to the emergency containment rig. Nearby, Arjun crouched next to a scorched server tower, hacking an interface that flickered with glitchy lines of code. Nathan and Crane were across the room, hustling to secure the jammed metal doors before the next reality wave fractured them completely from existence. Grice stood sentry, weapon in hand, painfully aware that his bullets would be useless against what they were facing—the fracturing of time.

In the center of it all, shining with an almost malevolent radiance, hung the Seal—its housing half-cracked, the quantum containment field flickering dangerously as if deciding whether to fail outright or lash out again. Small arcs of brilliant blue and white leaped across the gap in the containment—evidence of the artifact's raw power.

Across the broken lab, Dr. Thorne busily wrangled a specialized console. Her posture was unnervingly poised despite the surrounding chaos. Margaret hovered by Thorne's side, still clutching her tablet. The circles under Margaret's eyes had deepened in the last hour, dark half-moons betraying her exhaustion. She looked from Iris to Thorne and back again, her trembling lips pressed in a silent attempt to hold herself together.

Iris forced herself toward the battered center console. Each footstep felt less steady than the last, either from fear or the electromagnetic energy. "Is it still fracturing?" she rasped. Her throat was scratchy from inhaling eighteenth-century gun smoke.

"Worse than ever," Claire managed. Sweat beaded on her forehead as her nimble fingers keyed in fresh overrides to keep the last bits of power from blowing every fuse in the system.

Arjun swallowed, his voice dropping. "If we don't shut this down, we risk permanent tears in the timeline with eras bleeding into each other."

"We can't just shut it down," Thorne snapped. Her silver hair floated around her face from the quantum distortions. "If we kill the power, the quantum integration fails abruptly. The resulting void might tear a hole in space-time bigger than any controlled anomaly we've seen." Her voice quivered with the steely resolve of someone who had once believed—truly believed—that she was doing the right thing.

Margaret's voice wavered. "But we can't leave it like this. Every reading is trending upward. Each fracturing event is bigger and more stable." She shot Iris a haunted look. "We have to do something."

Iris could still feel Fort Ticonderoga's summer heat on her skin, but the current threat turned that heat into a fever. She looked at the Seal pulsing with terrifying potential, recalling the final moments of the Hessian Horseman, who had died centuries ago, and she wondered if that was her fate.

Jackson came alongside Iris, brushing a reassuring hand down her back. "We've got to decouple the Seal from the quantum system without triggering a meltdown." He turned to Claire and Arjun. "How can we do that?"

Claire slipped the last cable into place and tapped out a frantic series of commands. "We're flying blind here. The system is so integrated that it behaves like a single entity with the Seal at its heart."

Arjun rose to his full height, pushing his glasses up his nose. "Then we need someone who can sense what's happening inside." He glanced toward Margaret and then back to Jackson. "Emma. If she's like Iris described

—able to feel temporal anomalies—she might be able to guide us through this without unraveling everything."

Margaret's grip on her tablet slackened in recognition. She blinked. "Emma's locked up in the lower-level containment cell."

A fresh crack reverberated through the lab. Sparks flared in a corner, causing everyone to flinch as an entire cluster of monitors short-circuited.

"Take me there," Jackson urged Margaret. "We don't have much time."

Grice tested the weight of his sidearm. "I'll go with you and Margaret. Security's probably half-crazy from the temporal distortions, so we'll need some muscle." He glanced at Crane, who gave him a curt nod of approval.

Jackson turned to Crane. "Coordinate with Arjun and Claire. Keep us informed and continue trying to stabilize the lab to buy us some time." He lowered his voice. "Watch Thorne. I don't trust her, but we also can't do this without her command codes."

Iris started to leave with the others, but Arjun said gently, "We need you to stay. You and Jackson are the only ones with real experience handling the Seal itself. We might need one of you here."

Before Iris could respond, Jackson firmly said, "No." He reached for her hand. "You're staying with me. I'm not going to lose you again." He led her by the hand, and followed closely by Margaret, they hurried out of the lab's main doors, leaving behind the frantic glow of the Seal.

Another jarring ripple surged through the corridors. This time, the overhead lights shifted from harsh modern fluorescents to flickering lanterns in wrought-iron holders. The hall itself seemed older for an instant, the walls made of concrete rather than sterile white tile. Then it snapped back to the present, leaving everyone gasping.

As they walked, Jackson said, "Tell us everything."

Margaret cleared her throat. "They realized early on that Emma had a unique electromagnetic hypersensitivity. She could detect quantum fluctuations before they fully manifested. The Horsemen called her their 'quantum sensor.' They designed a specialized chamber in the sub-levels to amplify her electromagnetic sensitivity to quantum fluctuations, giving them advance notice whenever the Seal was about to cause a spike." A flicker of guilt crossed her face. "When I found out, I tried to remove her, but Eleanor—" She paused, swallowing hard. "She used my daughter as leverage to keep me in line."

Iris's heart clenched. "Tell us about the cell. What's the best way to break in?"

For a moment, Margaret's fear was palpable. Then she squared her shoulders, a spark of maternal ferocity breaking through her worn façade. "There's a code. I've watched them enough that I'm sure I know it, but it's always been too heavily guarded to try it. But even with the code, if any loyal Horsemen remain, they won't let Emma go easily."

"That's a risk we'll take," Jackson said firmly.

At the foot of the stairs, Margaret pressed a code into a flickering keypad. The door slid open on shaky rails. "Down here," she whispered as she stepped onto a steel-grated catwalk that wound around the building's perimeter.

Grice took the lead with his gun drawn, followed closely by Margaret, then Jackson and Iris. Overhead pipes groaned ominously while flickers of different historical eras layered over the sleek metal walls. A brass candelabra's ghostly flame flickered before blinking out of existence. For a heartbeat, a battered 1950s soda machine stood against the wall before vanishing.

Every nerve in Iris's body screamed in protest at each shifting timeline, but she forced herself onward to keep up with Jackson's determined stride.

Grice halted sharply and held up a hand. Around the bend, two armed guards stood watch in front of a thick steel door.

Margaret's eyes darted around. "Emma's cell is behind that door." Her voice trembled with emotion.

Judging by the white-knuckled grips on their rifles and the sweat glistening on their foreheads, the temporal surges had rattled the guards badly.

Grice breathed, "We need to subdue them quietly, or we risk raising the alarm."

Jackson slipped behind a structural pillar and edged closer to the guards. Iris's heart pounded so loudly she thought they would hear it. Grice gestured for Margaret to stay back, then advanced in a low crouch. Iris hung back, watching Jackson with her mind tracing each move, ready to leap to his aid. She wasn't a martial artist or a soldier, but she'd grown accustomed to danger over the past few weeks. She would do what she had to.

Grice gave Jackson a quick signal, and Jackson nodded. Springing around the corner, they seized the moment—Grice landed a sharp blow to the first guard's wrist, forcing the rifle from his grip, while Jackson tackled the second guard. The second guard twisted, nearly striking Jackson with an elbow, but Jackson ducked and pinned the man's arms. Meanwhile, the first guard managed to throw the older Grice off with overpowering strength.

Iris rushed in, ignoring the swirl of panic. She snatched the fallen rifle and flipped it around. She had no idea if it was loaded or if the safety was off, but the threat alone might help.

"Stop!" she shouted at the first guard, using a commanding voice she barely recognized as her own.

He froze for half a second, uncertain whether to laugh at the woman gripping his rifle or take her seriously. That half-second was all Grice needed to deliver a precisely aimed punch to the man's jaw, dropping him. The scuffle was over. Both men lay on the floor, unconscious or close to it.

Panting, Jackson looked up at Iris, eyebrows raised. "What was that?"

A shaky laugh escaped her. "My badass bitch voice."

A ghost of a grin flickered across Jackson's face, though worry lingered in his eyes.

Margaret approached the door they'd been guarding. A small keypad displayed a red light. With trembling fingers, she entered a code. The light turned green, and a heavy clunk signaled that the door was unlocking.

Together, they pushed it open and stepped into a chamber that made Iris's stomach drop. The room was dominated by a large glass enclosure tinted a faint violet, surrounded by thick cables and multiple monitoring panels. At the very center, a young woman sat on a small cot with her knees drawn up against her chest. She looked barely out of her teens, resembling a younger version of Margaret, with her mother's hazel eyes and delicate bone structure.

"Emma!" Margaret exclaimed. She stepped forward, but a second glass wall stood in her way. Through the partition, her daughter looked up, her eyes widening.

"Mom!" Emma's voice came muffled through the glass. Her face was pale, and dark bruises circled her wrists as if someone had been drawing blood or connecting IV lines.

Iris's heart clenched. The sight of a frightened young woman used as a living "barometer" hammered home just how inhumane this operation was.

Margaret ran her palm across the glass, tears streaming down her cheeks. "Sweetheart, I'm here. We're getting you out."

EIGHTEEN

Jackson pressed his palm against the thick reinforced glass of the holding cell, desperate to think of a solution. Through the transparent barrier, Emma looked frighteningly small, like a bird caught in an invisible net.

"Emma." He kept his voice steady and professional. "Can you hear me?"

She stirred, her movements sluggish but deliberate. "I can hear you," she managed, each word clearly an effort. "And...others. So many others. From before and the future."

Iris stepped closer. "Emma, we're going to get you out of here."

Jackson ran his hands through his hair in frustration. "There has to be a way—"

But Iris was already moving, her attention caught by something in the corner. She strode toward the red emergency cabinet set into the wall. "Jackson, help me with this."

He turned, momentarily confused, then understood as she wrenched open the cabinet door and pulled out a heavy industrial-grade fire extinguisher. Not elegant, perhaps, but sometimes the simplest solutions were best.

"This is reinforced glass," he said, quickly assessing its considerable thickness. "But it's still just glass. If we hit it at the right point—"

"Precisely." Iris hefted the extinguisher and handed it to Jackson. "Emma, get back from the window. As far as you can."

Emma pressed herself against the far wall, hands pressed to the concrete. Fear and hope warred in her expression.

Jackson swung the extinguisher toward the glass. The impact sent a spiderweb of cracks racing across the surface, accompanied by an ominous crackle of energy.

"Let's try that again." Jackson swung once more, and this time, the glass shattered inward. Fragments rained down as temporal energy sparked and fizzled around the jagged edges.

"Emma!" Iris called as she reached through the opening. "Take my hand!"

Emma lunged forward and caught Iris's outstretched hand. The moment they touched, a shock rippled through them both—not painful, but disorienting, as if they'd briefly touched every possible version of themselves across a thousand timelines.

Jackson cleared the rest of the broken glass.

As soon as Emma was through, Margaret rushed to her. "I've got you," she cried, wrapping her arms around her daughter. The reunion was brief but fierce, weeks of worry compressed into a single embrace.

Emma sagged against her mother, but her eyes remained alert, darting around the corridor. "We need to go," she said. "The containment systems are failing. All of them. And the Seal..." She shuddered. "It's awake now."

Jackson met Iris's gaze. "Let's get back to the lab," he said, already calculating their best route through the chaos above. "The rest of the team will have to handle the Seal till we get there."

They made their way back through the corridors, weaving around broken pipes and half-collapsed archways. Once, they had to stop to fend off confused guards, but the others had fled in the meltdown of temporal chaos.

Finally, they reached the stairway that led to the lab. Emma staggered and gripped the railing while Margaret circled her daughter's waist and guided her along.

"I'm sorry," Emma said softly as she leaned against her mother's shoulder. Her eyes fluttered shut. "This was all because I—"

Margaret shushed her. "No. None of this is your fault. I got involved with them for the best reasons, but they took advantage. I'm so sorry."

"You wanted to help me. Protect me," Emma

murmured, forcing a small, heartbreaking smile. "I know, Mom. I know."

They worked their way along the flickering fluorescent-lit corridor at the top of the stairs. The view through the windows was barely recognizable. Half-spindly trees lined a muddy nineteenth-century wagon path while distant calls of "Whoa there!" mingled with the mechanical hum of the facility's failing lights.

"Come on," Jackson urged, forging ahead. "We're close."

They rounded a corner and emerged in the lab's main control room. Technicians scrambled about. Some shouted in confusion while others stared blankly at the swirling distortions overhead. Arjun, Claire, Crane, and Nathan were huddled by the primary quantum console. With each beep, the graphs soared further into the danger zone.

Claire spotted them first. "You did it!" she gasped. Relief shone in her eyes as she rushed forward and helped Margaret guide Emma to a stool.

"We have minutes—maybe seconds—until the system hits critical mass," Arjun reported with a trembling voice. "We tried to run a partial disconnection of the Seal, but the feedback was insane. Thorne claims a full meltdown is guaranteed if we do. But if we don't..."

He didn't need to finish. At the center of the lab, the Seal continued to spin in its containment cylinder, arcs of crackling energy lashing out at the quantum hardware. Every time a spark jumped from the Seal to the equipment, the entire facility groaned, reverberating with the force of colliding timelines.

Jackson studied Emma, who was leaning heavily against Margaret. "Can you sense how to disconnect the Seal safely?" he suggested.

Thorne replied, "She can feel the anomalies before they spike. But that doesn't mean—"

"I can try," Emma whispered as she shut her eyes. "I just need...a minute."

Claire supported her from the other side. "Take your time, Emma. Focus. We'll manage the data you give us."

Margaret smoothed her daughter's hair. "I'll be right here."

A stillness fell over the lab despite the sounding alarms and sizzling sparks. Everyone's eyes were on Emma as she inhaled deeply. She pressed her palms together and then separated them slowly as if feeling the invisible threads of time in the air.

A soft gasp escaped her lips. "It's...so strong," she breathed, furrowing her brow. "Like a thousand quantum frequencies resonating at once. But there's a pattern in the electromagnetic field."

Arjun perched behind a console, ready to input commands. Claire hovered over the quantum interface, her usual professional distance cracking to reveal genuine concern. Nathan stood guard at the perimeter, weapon in hand, warily eyeing the swirling illusions that threatened to break through. Crane placed a firm hand on Thorne's shoulder, not in comfort, but as a warning not to interfere.

Emma stood motionless until Jackson wondered if she was all right. Then her eyes snapped open with sudden clarity.

"It's the pulses," she said, her voice rough but certain. "Small bursts at five-second intervals, followed by a stabilizing jolt to anchor the quantum states." She winced, pressing fingers to her temple. "After that, we can separate the Seal. But—" She glanced up, tears in her eyes. "You'll have to physically remove it at the exact moment the quantum field drops below the threshold."

"I'll do it," Jackson said immediately.

Arjun pointed toward the personal protective equipment changing room. "Put on a protective suit. It's quantum-shielded to protect against the electromagnetic emissions, but the temporal energy is still a wild card."

Jackson grabbed the suit and undid the fasteners, but a problem was immediately apparent. "It's too small," he said, frustration evident in the tight set of his jaw. "Damn it, it's sized for—"

"For me," Iris finished, already moving forward. Her heart hammered against her ribs, but her voice remained steady. "I'll get the Seal."

"Absolutely not." Jackson caught her wrist. "Iris, I can't let you—"

"Let me?" She met his gaze, but the fear in his eyes softened her initial annoyance.

He released her wrist and took hold of her shoulders. "There has to be another way."

"There isn't," Emma called out, her voice strained. "And we're running out of time!"

Iris stepped closer to Jackson and looked straight into his eyes with a confidence she didn't really feel. "I'll be fine."

His expression shifted to one of resignation. "Be careful," he said roughly. "Please."

She managed a small smile. "I always am." Then, she turned and put on the suit.

"Arjun," Claire shouted. "Now or never!"

With frantic keystrokes, they initiated the partial shutdown Emma had described. The humming pitch of the quantum system grew shrill, like metal screeching under stress. Emma tracked the quantum fluctuations, calling out each moment the electromagnetic field stabilized enough for the next pulse while Claire hammered in the commands. Arjun worked the stabilizer. His movements were precise despite the chaos around them.

Jackson's eyes never left Iris's suited form while Margaret clung to her daughter's hand.

"Hold on, Emma. Hold on." The words seemed to carry the weight of years—all the times Margaret had held her daughter through illness, fear, and loss.

At Emma's signal, Iris stepped up to the containment field. The Seal hovered, spinning, arcs of unnatural lightning dancing around it. The suit seemed to be doing its job, but still, the electromagnetic energy made her skin crawl.

Emma cried out, "Now! The field's low enough—reach in and pull it free!"

Iris lunged forward and gripped the artifact. It felt heavier than she'd expected, as if it carried the weight of every historical moment within it. Through her protective gloves, she felt its warmth and the subtle vibrations of power.

Jackson watched, his mind spinning with fleeting images—Washington crossing the Delaware, Colonial farmsteads, modern city streets, even a flash of a Hessian soldier riding valiantly. His muscles tensed with the need to go to Iris to protect her, but he forced himself to stay back.

Iris lifted the Seal from its cradle. Then, everything went eerily silent.

NINETEEN

Reality snapped as the quantum field collapsed in on itself. A thunderous boom reverberated through the lab, sending everyone staggering. Iris fell back, still clutching the Seal, but Jackson's steadying hands gripped her shoulders. Sparks hammered against the metal cage of the chamber until, with a final shriek, the lights blinked out, leaving them in total darkness.

Jackson's ears rang as he held a trembling Iris. Emergency lights flickered back on, casting the scene in surreal shadows. Iris was on her knees in the chamber, carefully securing the Seal in its protective container, her movements laborious yet precise. When she finished, Nathan steadied them both as they rose to join Crane and Grice, who stood in stunned silence. Emma slumped into her mother's arms, completely drained but alive.

The fear Jackson had been suppressing now overwhelmed him. He called out to Iris as two technicians guided her toward the protective gear changing room.

Thorne said, "Calm down, Wilde. She'll be back as soon as she's out of that suit. The quantum shielding needs to be properly deactivated." Her voice had lost its earlier edge of desperation and settled into a tone closer to professional exhaustion.

Jackson turned to Arjun, who nodded reassuringly. "She'll be fine." But his words did little to calm Jackson.

The Seal, now secured in its protective container, sat innocuously on a cart. Jackson looked from it to Arjun and Claire. "What happens to it now?" His voice was steady, but his eyes kept straying to the quantum containment chamber door.

Claire adjusted her readings, her movements precise despite her obvious fatigue. "It'll need specialized quantum containment—something that can shield both its electromagnetic emissions and prevent any quantum fluctuations."

Jackson stared, his heart pounding. "Iris disconnected it. Shouldn't that be enough?"

Claire's eyebrows furrowed. "I want to say yes, but we're in uncharted territory. I'd rather we kept it isolated just to be safe."

She glanced at Arjun, and he nodded, confirming.

As his pulse slowed back to normal, Jackson became more aware of his surroundings. In the corridor beyond, water dripped from a burst pipe, while inside the room, a console sizzled. But the swirling illusions of other eras were gone, and the distorted quantum resonance of colliding time streams was now replaced by the subtle hum of stabilizing reality.

A door slid open, and Iris emerged, having shed her protective gear. Relief shone from her eyes, along with the brilliant, quietly triumphant smile that had first caught Jackson's attention.

He rushed to her side, propriety forgotten in the aftermath of the crisis, and pulled her into an embrace. "You did it," he breathed. "And thank God, it's over."

Iris's hand found his. "Not quite how I'd prefer to impress you," she murmured.

"Oh? And what exactly would you prefer?" The words came easily, despite everything—or perhaps because of it. Near-death experiences had a way of clarifying priorities.

She leaned closer. "I was thinking maybe a presentation about quantum mechanics and temporal theory. Over dinner?" Her twinkling eyes met his.

"That's a hard no on the presentation, but dinner? Absolutely." He drew her closer and planted a kiss on her forehead.

Emma's voice cut through their moment. "The quantum fluctuations," she said, sitting taller and glancing about. "They're stabilizing. The electromagnetic field is smoothing out like ripples in a pond." Her eyes were clearer now, more focused. "It worked. We really did it."

Claire was already typing less furiously as she studied her screen. "Quantum readings are stabilizing. No more quantum disruptions or anomalous electromagnetic signatures." She stopped typing and looked up, relaxing her shoulders. She turned to Arjun, who stopped typing and looked into Claire's eyes. Neither moved for a moment.

"We did it," she whispered.

"Yeah," Arjun said.

Claire ripped off her headset, hurled it aside, and then lunged at Arjun and kissed him. After a moment to recover, Arjun kissed her back—with more passion than anyone present expected from him.

In an instant, he came to his senses, pulled away, and looked about at the others in the room. "Sorry."

"I'm not," Claire said. With that, she gathered her headset and wrapped up the cord as though nothing had happened.

Thorne cleared her throat to draw their attention. She seemed smaller somehow, stripped of her usual authority by the day's events. "The Seal will need to be secured. There are protocols—"

"Which we'll follow," Crane interrupted smoothly, "after everyone's had a chance to rest and recover." His tone left no room for argument, and Thorne acquiesced, perhaps resigned to the fact that her moment of control over the Seal had passed.

Margaret helped Emma to her feet and supported her daughter with gentle determination. "Come on, sweetheart. Let's get you checked out properly." She paused, looking back at Jackson and Iris. "Thank you. Both of you. For everything."

Emma managed a tired smile. "Maybe next time we can just meet for coffee? Without all the drama?"

"Deal," Iris said, returning the smile. She watched them go, struck by how ordinary they appeared despite the extraordinary day they'd all had.

※

AFTER THE QUANTUM systems were powered down and the Seal secured, Thorne remained in her office, methodically deleting files while the others handled the cleanup. Jackson found her there with her silver hair disheveled. Her polished academic facade was cracked to reveal a rare glimpse of her vulnerable side.

"I wondered when you'd show up," she said without looking up. "To demand answers? Or maybe revenge?"

Jackson leaned against the doorframe. "I want to understand. You were brilliant, Eleanor. Respected. What made this worth throwing it all away?"

She stopped typing, her hands trembling slightly. "Did you know I had a brother?"

Jackson shook his head.

She smiled faintly. "Michael. He was a theoretical physicist—brilliant, idealistic. He discovered something in his research about parallel timelines and quantum entanglement on a macro scale. But no one would fund his work. Too fantastic, they said." Her voice turned bitter. "He died thinking he was a failure with his life's work dismissed as pseudoscience."

"And then you found the Seal," Jackson said quietly.

"Not just found it. I understood what it meant. Everything Michael theorized—it was all there. It was true. The Seal proved it." She looked up. Her eyes were bright with a desperate kind of certainty. "We weren't just studying history. We were going to rewrite it. Make it better. Prevent wars, save lives... Maybe even Michael's."

"By controlling time itself? That kind of power—"

"Would be dangerous in the wrong hands?" She laughed bitterly. "Of course it would. That's why it had to be us. Scientists. Scholars. People who understood the responsibility."

Jackson studied her face—the dark circles under her eyes, the slight tremor in her hands.

"I started seeing alternate timelines—versions of Michael—where he lived, where he worked. I couldn't stop." Her expression crumpled. "By the time it all spun out of control, we were too far gone."

Jackson barely recognized the brilliant professional he once knew. Seeing her like this filled him with pity. "So, what now?"

Thorne gestured at her computer and typed some more keystrokes. "I'm eliminating every trace of our research. It's too dangerous to exist, even in theory."

Jackson nodded. It went without saying that none of this could get out to the public without bringing dangerous attention to the Seal. "What if someone on your staff talks?"

She stopped typing and turned to face him. "I'm deleting it all and scrubbing the drive. No one will find—or worse, try to replicate—what went on here. If anyone talks, they'll be viewed, like my brother, as eccentric conspiracy theorists."

"What will you do?"

Thorne's smile was sad. "Resign from the university. Cite health reasons—time with my family, the usual lies. Maybe move somewhere quiet." She met his gaze. "You don't have to worry. I won't try again."

Jackson nodded slowly. "The Wardens will be watching."

"I know." She turned back to her computer. "Give my regards to my friends at Columbia. Tell them... Never mind. It's better if I just fade away into the sunset." She rolled her eyes and chuckled.

Jackson nodded. There was nothing more to say or do. Once again, it would be up to the Wardens to protect the Seal and ensure it upheld the ideals for which it was intended.

As Jackson left Thorne's office, he glanced back one last time. Eleanor Thorne sat straight-backed at her desk, dignity intact even in defeat, systematically erasing all evidence of her greatest mistake. She would disappear into academic obscurity, but her cautionary tale would remain with the Wardens—a reminder that even the noblest of intentions could be corrupted by the power to pursue it.

THE LAB slowly emptied as various team members departed. Soon, only Jackson and Iris remained, standing in the aftermath of their impossible day.

Iris started to follow the others out of the lab, but Jackson gently pulled her back inside. "Iris." Despite being flooded with feelings, he struggled to find the right words. "Watching someone you care about disappear into another century is…painful."

"Being catapulted into a historic battle isn't all that fun, either." Iris arched an eyebrow, even as she leaned slightly into his touch.

As Iris slid her free hand up to rest against his chest, Jackson was acutely aware of his pounding heartbeat. His words came out slowly. "What I'm trying to say is…"

Without waiting, Iris said, "Me, too," and kissed him.

Abandoning all hope of talking, Jackson unleashed his heart with a deepening kiss.

When they finally parted, the lab's emergency lights had dimmed to a soft glow, casting everything in gentle shadows. Outside, the facility hummed with the normal sounds of cleanup and recovery, but in this moment between them, it felt as though time held its breath.

At the end of a day full of temporal chaos, they had found their own perfect moment.

TWENTY

Twilight settled over the hills like a worn blanket. Through the cabin's great room windows, Iris watched darkness overtake the sky as pinpoints of starlight came into view. As close as they'd come to a temporal disaster, it was oddly comforting now to watch life go on as it always had.

Behind Iris, the team had settled into various poses of exhausted relief around the room. Margaret's daughter curled against her mother on the oversized couch. Emma still looked pale, but some of her usual spark had returned—enough that she teased Nathan about his "old man noises" when he claimed the room's best armchair.

"I heard that," Nathan grumbled, but his eyes sparkled with genuine warmth. "Just because some of us have earned our battle scars—"

"Speaking of battle scars," Claire interrupted from her perch on the hearth, "we should discuss the Seal's containment. Arjun and I have looked into secure storage at a few of the area research labs."

Iris felt Jackson move beside her at the window. His shoulder brushed against hers, a casual touch that sent awareness skittering down her spine. "No," he said quickly.

Arjun shot a surprised look at Jackson. "But it obviously needs special handling—and strong security."

Claire nodded. "We don't want a repeat of the Horsemen affair."

Nathan leaned forward and said firmly, "Crane and I will take care of the storage."

Arjun's eyes widened, but no one argued the point, which was clearly settled.

"But we should address the Horsemen. Dr. Thorne's team has scattered, effectively disbanding the Horsemen, but tales will be told—not that I expect anyone to believe a band of Revolutionary War soldiers marched through a temporal fracture. Still, more than ever, we'll need to be vigilant," Nathan added.

"Of course." Jackson glanced around at the others. "We'll do all we can."

"I hoped you'd feel that way." Nathan looked straight at Jackson. "Because I've decided it's time for me to step back from field operations."

"Dad—" Jackson started.

Nathan held up a hand. "Let me finish. I've had my time in the field. I've watched you grow from a boy who memorized battle formations to a man who can handle temporal chaos without losing his head—or his heart." His voice roughened.

The silence that followed held years of unspoken emotions—duty, worry, and love. Jackson swallowed hard. "I learned from the best."

"Pfft." Nathan waved away the sentiment, but his eyes were suspiciously bright. "You learned from books and experience—and people who challenged you to be better." His brief glance at Iris was meaningful. "Anyway, we'll talk more."

Iris could see that Jackson was deeply moved, but beyond that, she could only imagine his thoughts. Nathan had all but passed the torch to him, but she couldn't guess whether he'd want to accept it.

"Speaking of challenges," Margaret said, her fingers combing absently through Emma's hair, "we should discuss Emma's abilities. Now that they're not being artificially amplified—"

"I can still feel them," Emma said quietly. "Like echoes. But it's different now. My electromagnetic sensitivity isn't being amplified anymore. It's like... hearing music from another room instead of being trapped in the middle of an orchestra's brass section."

Margaret fixed sympathetic eyes on her daughter. "I'm reluctant to subject her to testing, but I'm concerned about the toll this has taken on her."

Emma placed her hand on her mother's. "I won't be a lab rat." She turned to Jackson and Iris. "But you've all done so much for me. If there's anything I can ever do..." Overcome with emotion, she simply nodded.

Knowing looks rippled through the room. Claire's hand found Arjun's, and Margaret pulled Emma closer. Jackson's fingers brushed Iris's wrist—a touch so light it might have been accidental if not for the way his thumb traced her pulse point.

"There are still loose ends," Arjun said, though he didn't move away from Claire. "Thorne's handling the facility cleanup."

"Yeah, she messaged us that she's working on a cover story—something about the abandoned military radar tower, UFO sightings, and rumors of an alien abduction," Jackson said.

Iris's jaw dropped for a moment before she smiled. "Actually, it sounds crazy enough to work."

Jackson nodded, agreeing.

Iris's imagination started to run wild. "All we need are some ghost-investigating college students on break to make YouTube videos about it to deflect from what really happened."

Jackson chuckled. "Problem solved."

"If you two are quite finished," Nathan said, his gruff tone belying his obvious affection, "what's next for everyone?"

"Back to school and, fingers crossed, normal life," Emma replied.

Margaret's smile faded as she turned to Nathan. "I have a meeting set up at the Heritage Center to discuss my return. I've explained as best as I could that there was a family crisis. They're willing to talk, so that's a start."

"I have some irons in the fire," Grice added, remaining deliberately vague.

Crane shot him a disapproving look. "I'll continue as I have been, supporting the Wardens."

Suppressing a grin, Arjun said, "So that leaves Jackson and Iris." He raised his eyebrows and peered at them expectantly. "Any plans for you two?"

Iris blushed, and Jackson's lips moved to form words that didn't quite come out.

"Oh, come on," Claire laughed. "You two are pathetic."

"Please," Nathan muttered, though he smiled as he pushed himself out of his chair. "Before we lapse into full-blown junior high, I could use some coffee." With that, he headed for the kitchen.

The group began to disperse. Claire and Arjun went to the porch to check the weather, or so they said. Crane retreated to his laptop to update his Warden's journal, and Margaret and Emma headed to the kitchen for coffee and snacks.

Jackson turned to Iris, still holding her wrist. "Care to join me? The view from the back deck is spectacular at night."

"Subtle," she murmured but took his offered arm.

"I never claimed subtlety as one of my talents." He guided her out to the deck, where he lit the gas fireplace. "Though I do have other qualities that might recommend me."

"Oh?" She stepped outside and leaned against the railing. "Such as?"

He stepped closer. "Such as a thorough understanding of the importance of timing." He moved even closer. "And an appreciation for seizing the moment."

"I'm listening," Iris breathed.

His kiss felt like coming home to a place she'd always longed for—familiar, thrilling, and right. When they finally parted, the stars seemed brighter as if stretching across time to shine down on this perfect moment.

Inside, they could hear the others laughing, their voices weaving together like threads in a tapestry. Tomorrow would bring new challenges, new questions, and new adventures. But for now, on this deck, at this moment, they had all the time in the world.

TWENTY-ONE

Iris and Jackson stood on the Sleepy Hollow Bridge, watching the water flowing below. Iris thought it would be easier to talk here than at the cottage, but she regretted the choice now as memories came flooding back.

She swallowed, wishing she'd found the right words. It wasn't for lack of thought. She'd imagined this scene in a dozen different ways, but none of them ever felt right.

"I'm leaving," she said quietly, glancing away.

Jackson stared at her in stunned disbelief. "Leaving?"

"Moving." He looked so confused, so she tried to be clearer. "Away."

"But I thought we were...something."

"I know. And I don't want to leave you." Iris's stomach sank.

Jackson's expression flickered from confusion to shock. "Then don't."

She took an uneasy breath and let it out. "I've been offered a job. It's perfect for me, really—a small college. Instructor to start with, but after the first year, I'll be considered for a tenure-track position."

He stared blankly.

Iris couldn't bear the silence. "It's in the Midwest. Peaceful and quiet."

"Yeah, cornfields are like that. What the hell are you talking about?"

His voice was so loud that Iris leaned back. "It's what I wanted"—she gestured weakly—"before all of this happened."

He mimicked her gesture. "But all of this did happen. We happened!" He struggled for words. "I guess I thought that changed things. It changed me."

In the lamplight, she caught a glimpse of pure, unguarded pain on his face as he said, "So, you've accepted it...obviously. Without even telling me you were in the running?"

"I applied for some jobs before I ever met you. And then, it was kind of out of the blue. I got a call and had a Zoom interview."

Jackson asked quietly, "When?"

"Before all the Seal stuff escalated." She sighed. "I didn't mention it because I didn't think I'd actually get it." She hesitated. "And I didn't want to be embarrassed when I didn't."

"Embarrassed?" He looked at her as if she were a stranger.

She almost wished he would yell because his hurt stare was painful. So she did the only thing she could do to break the silence. "To be honest, I'd practically forgotten about it. I mean, I didn't forget exactly. I just didn't think I'd get it," she said softly. "But I did. Yesterday."

The dark, hopeless look in his eyes broke her.

She stared into the distance—anywhere but at Jackson. "I mean, come on, Jackson, what's there for me here?"

He shot her a sharp look.

"I mean besides you."

His eyes flared with anger.

Iris clenched and then flexed her hands. "That's not what I meant. Of course, you're here—and you know how I feel about you."

A bitter laugh bubbled up to the surface. "I thought I did."

Nothing was coming out right. "Put yourself in my place. My job at the Heritage Center is over."

"Because you quit."

Iris's anger flared. "I quit because I couldn't conduct tours while we were chasing the Cassandra Collective and the Horsemen all over upstate New York. Besides, I worked my butt off to get a doctorate so I could work as a historian. You, of all people, should understand that. Can you honestly say you'd be content as a tour guide when your passion is elsewhere?"

"My passion is you," he murmured. "Which, I guess, will be elsewhere," he added bitterly.

His words sent a physical pang through her heart and tears to her eyes. "Jackson, I love you."

"I can tell."

"If it were you, would you give up your job and stay home while I worked?"

When he didn't answer, Iris pressed on. "Because if you would, then quit your job and come with me."

Jackson's voice boomed. "That's not fair."

"No, it's not."

She watched the tension tighten in Jackson's posture. She could hear the effort he was making to keep his voice even. "Look...I get that you need a job, Iris. I do. It's just... I guess I thought we'd talk about it. Make a plan."

She bit her lip, hating the flicker of disappointment in his eyes. "Sleepy Hollow was always meant to be temporary for me," she said gently. "You knew that. Then everything spiraled into something bigger." She paused with her voice catching. "And so did we."

He nodded hopelessly and then said softly, as though he still couldn't quite believe it, "So I guess that's it. After all we've been through, you're just... done?"

She swallowed hard. "I start in the first summer session. But I've got to find a place to live, move, and put together my course materials—you know."

Jackson gave a slight nod, looking completely defeated.

Iris couldn't help feeling like he didn't quite understand. "If I stayed, what would I do? Wait for the next Warden crisis or conspiracy to show up?"

Jackson shrugged. "I thought we made a pretty good team."

They had, and that was what made it so difficult. "We did, but I'm just not ready to move in and be just a professor's girlfriend."

Jackson's face flickered with something between shock and confusion. "We've nearly died for each other —and I'd do it for you again because I love you, Iris. I love you! So, if that makes you just a professor's girlfriend..." He shook his head without finishing.

Iris closed her eyes for a moment, but the heartache was impossible to block out. She forced herself to look into his eyes. "I love you, too." Then she released a shaky breath. "But that's not always enough."

His gaze turned cold. "Why not?"

The question hung in the air. Iris couldn't trust her voice, so she shook her head slowly and blinked back tears. "I'm sorry." The night suddenly felt darker and colder.

Slowly, Jackson closed the distance between them and drew her into his arms. Iris surrendered to his warmth and strength, leaning against his chest to breathe in his scent one last time.

He drew back, cupping her face in his hands, his thumbs brushing her cheeks. When he pressed a soft, lingering kiss to her forehead, she was nearly undone.

"Stay safe," he murmured, his voice thick with emotion.

She managed a shaky smile. "You too."

Stepping apart made her feel as if she had torn something priceless in two that would never be mended. Turning, Iris walked away into the foggy gloom illuminated by the lamplight. Each step on the frozen sidewalk felt heavy, making the distance between them absolute.

Half a block later, she couldn't help herself. She looked back. He was standing in the same spot as though he hoped she might change her mind.

As she turned the corner, an unexpected sound sent a shiver down her spine—the thunder of horse hooves. She froze. Her heart pounded. Across the street, through a trick of moonlight and fog, a spectral figure on horseback emerged from the mist. His form flickered, appearing half real and half illusion, as the steed's hooves barely skimmed the ground. The Horseman—silent guardian of legend and time.

They faced one another as if sharing a breathless instant. Iris's heart skipped a beat. This was the same Hessian soldier—or his ghost—who had helped her across a fractured timeline. He'd saved her. But why appear now? Whether this was a warning or blessing, she couldn't decide. Or maybe it was simply a haunting reminder of what she was leaving behind.

As quickly as he'd appeared, he was gone, fading into the shadows beneath the trees' skeletal branches.

The night returned to its empty stillness, broken only by the sound of her ragged breathing.

Iris pulled her coat tighter around her and forced herself to keep walking.

DAYS LATER: The Heritage Center

Sunlight streamed through the expansive windows of the Heritage Center, lighting motes of dust floating weightlessly in the air. Fewer visitors wandered about than usual, making the place feel oddly subdued. Outside, the snow had melted into a slushy mix, leaving patches of ice scattered throughout the courtyard. The crisis that had gripped Sleepy Hollow was over, but a subtle tension lingered in the air.

Iris stepped inside with a cardboard box tucked under one arm. A pang of nostalgia struck her. She'd walked these same halls countless times, giving tours and sharing her knowledge of historical lore. This place had been a refuge for her, but now, she was leaving. It was time.

Her footsteps echoed on the polished floor. Margaret Verplanck had asked her to drop by for a final chat and to gather whatever personal items remained at her old desk in the archives. Iris wove her way toward the staff corridor, pausing to look at a display she had helped curate—*Colonial Swords and Sabers*. She trailed her fingers across the glass, recalling the thrill of showcasing real artifacts from America's founding struggles.

Though the heart of her journey lay in Sleepy Hollow's unique mysteries, reality called her to a more ordinary and predictable life.

She whispered to herself, "Get in, say your goodbyes, and don't linger." Yet regret weighed her down with each passing minute.

At her office door, she found Margaret waiting, wearing a tired but warm smile. The older woman had changed so much in the weeks since the Horsemen's plan had unraveled. She looked freer, albeit haunted by guilt for her past complicity.

"Iris," Margaret said as she stepped forward to clasp her hand. "I'm so glad you came."

Iris managed a faint smile in return. "I wanted to see you before heading out," she said, lifting the box slightly. "I have a few office knickknacks and books to pick up, but mostly, I just wanted to thank you for everything."

Margaret lowered her eyes. Her voice was tinged with regret. "I owe you far more than thanks, Iris. You risked so much—" She took a breath and released it with a weary sigh. "It all worked out, more or less. I'm still dealing with the aftermath, but Emma's recovering." She brightened. "She's going back to college next semester, and the Center is moving forward with some new programs. I...I wish I could keep you here on staff."

Iris's smile turned sad. "I appreciate that. But...it's time." She swallowed.

Margaret patted Iris's hand. "I understand. If you

ever need anything, I'm here." Then her gaze flicked beyond Iris's shoulder to the corridor. "Oh—Jackson?"

The sound of his name was a jolt. She turned to see Jackson standing at the other end of the corridor, hands in his pockets. He wore that same leather jacket he had on when they first met—cool and collected as ever with those dark eyes that always made her heart weightless.

Jackson. Her heart twisted. She struggled to say his name. This couldn't be a coincidence. She recalled that Margaret had suggested this precise time. Margaret's sheepish glance between the two of them made it clear she had orchestrated the meeting. Iris knew she was trying to help, but she'd just caused more pain. And yet, it felt so good to see him.

Jackson approached with measured steps. His guarded gaze moved from Iris to Margaret. "Margaret, you...you said something about lunch?"

Margaret cleared her throat. "Yes. But I'm so sorry. Something came up. Perhaps another time, hmm?" She patted her blouse pockets, then dropped her arms. "Oh. I left my phone in the car." She grabbed her keys. "You two can...chat while I'm gone." With that, she left them alone in the office.

An awkward tension settled. Iris could practically feel the swirl of unspoken words coiling around them. Here she was face to face with the raw truth of her choices.

"You look...good," Jackson offered quietly, studying her. "How was your trip?"

Iris set the cardboard box on the table. "Fine. Just a

quick flight with one connection. I found an apartment near campus." A sudden apprehension gripped her stomach. "I leave in a week."

He nodded. His gaze dropped to the floor. "That soon?" It sounded more like an admission of defeat than a question.

She fiddled with the edge of the empty box. "Yeah. Classes start next month, but the department chair wants to help me get settled." She forced a smile that didn't reach her eyes. "I'm teaching American History."

"Good," he echoed, his brows knitting together. "I start my new semester in a couple of weeks, too. My father gave me boxes of old Warden business to sort through. That and a full teaching load will keep me... busy."

Iris tucked a loose strand of hair behind her ear. "Look, I-I'm sorry. I hope you understand it wasn't an easy decision."

Jackson's jaw clenched for a moment. Then he exhaled slowly. "It's your life, Iris." His voice was calm, but the effort cost him something. "I...want you to be happy."

She nodded. Her throat was tight. "Thanks. I just —" She could feel tears threatening to surface again but refused to let them. "I hope you know how much you meant—mean to me."

He nodded but averted his eyes. "Anyway, I, uh..." His eyebrows drew together. "Good luck."

Her heart, her stomach—everything ached. "Thanks."

For a moment, they stood there in the air thick with silent emotion. Then Iris opened her arms, and Jackson stepped in. It felt strangely cautious. All she wanted right now was to kiss him, but she buried her face pressed against his shoulder and inhaled his comforting scent, desperate to memorize it.

"Take care," he murmured as his hand stroked her back in a gentle motion.

"You too," she whispered with tears burning at the corners of her eyes.

As they pulled apart slowly, the loss of his warmth struck her with brutal clarity. Feeling cold and alone, she flashed a weak smile and swiped away the tears obscuring her vision. "I'm sure we'll...see each other again." But it wasn't a promise.

Jackson nodded stiffly. "Yeah."

He glanced at the cardboard box on the table and at Iris, then turned and headed down the corridor. Iris watched him as each footstep echoed through the empty hallway.

It's for the best. She closed her eyes and willed herself to feel calm and content.

But as Margaret returned moments later and quietly placed a hand on Iris's shoulder, the tears flowed.

"Some goodbyes leave a wound," Margaret said softly, "But you'll heal."

Margaret drew Iris into a sympathetic embrace. In the silent hallway of the Heritage Center, Iris gave in and let herself mourn.

TWENTY-TWO

It was late. Iris had drifted off while reading in her living room, surrounded by half-packed boxes and a lingering sense of unease. Ever since that final, painful farewell at the Heritage Center, she'd walked around in a daze, unsure whether her decision to leave Sleepy Hollow was the bravest or the most cowardly thing she'd ever done.

A faint knock on the door roused her from a light doze. She blinked, and her heart lurched at the thought of who might be calling at such an hour. Padding softly across the living room in her wool socks, she peered through the peephole—and her stomach twisted. It was Jackson. His silhouette was unmistakable under the dim corridor light.

For a moment, she hesitated. Letting him in would derail her desperate plans to maintain a boundary between them because each time she saw him, her heart broke all over again. But she couldn't ignore him or the thrill of seeing him. With her heart banging against her ribs, she quietly unbolted the door.

When she opened it, she nearly lost her nerve upon seeing the raw mix of hope and vulnerability on his face. He wore that damn jacket he looked so hot in. His shoulders were tense from the cold—or perhaps from the uncertainty of what he'd say next.

"Iris," he said simply. His voice was hushed so as not to disturb the neighbors.

She swallowed. "Jackson, it's late... Are you okay?"

He exhaled as though relieved that she'd even asked. "Yeah. I mean, no. I just...needed to see you." His gaze darted inside, taking in the boxes stacked near the door.

Their eyes locked, and tension crackled in the silence. Iris's pulse fluttered. "Do you, um...want to come in?" She forced the words out, even though part of her brain screamed, *Don't do it! You'll lose your resolve!*

He studied her, seeming to sense her fear. "Why don't we go for a walk?" he countered gently.

Relief and panic warred inside her. A walk would be less intimate, but then again, a walk was how everything had started, in a way. Exploring Sleepy Hollow's secrets had set them on a path that irrevocably changed both their lives.

She glanced at the slushy street outside and sighed. "Okay."

After she donned her jacket and boots, she locked the apartment, and they made their way onto the dimly lit sidewalks. Winter's chill lingered, but it wasn't as bitter as before. In fact, it was an unusually mild January night for Sleepy Hollow. Their breath formed small plumes in the crisp air as they walked in silence. After a block or two, it became clear where Jackson was leading them—the same route that curved around the old church, over the rolling hill, and past a grove of ancient trees.

Iris's heart kicked up a notch. She knew this path too well. It led toward the stone Horseman's Bridge. In the hush between them, she felt memories creeping back—dashing through these trees to save each other from the Cassandra Collective, the Wardens, the Horsemen, and the place where she'd broken the news that she was leaving. Too much had happened here.

When the bridge came into view, the moonlight outlined its graceful arches over the shallow, ice-rimmed creek. It was the same spot where local legends claimed countless sightings of the Headless Horseman —the place where their real-life nightmare had begun and somehow ended.

They stopped near the curved part of the railing, and the quiet of the night settled around them. Below, the water gurgled softly, half-choked by patches of ice. Bony tree branches stretched overhead as if reaching for the pale sliver of moon.

"I can't let you leave like this. Not without... without telling you something," Jackson said.

Iris tucked her hands into her coat pockets and braced herself. "Jackson..."

He nodded, his jaw clenched with apparent nerves.

"I know we've had this conversation, and I know what you've decided. But I had to see you."

She exhaled, wishing she knew what to say, but she barely knew what she felt anymore.

He glanced away. "There's something I...I haven't told you. My father is retiring from leadership of the Wardens." His voice was tight.

She nodded. "He said he was stepping back from field operations."

"Yes, but we talked yesterday, and he's decided to hand everything over to me."

She blinked. "Not just the field operations?"

He let out a strange laugh that lacked humor. "No. He's retiring from active duty, or so he claims. He wants me to take charge of the whole operation—the Seal, the old secrets, future threats—and more than I ever imagined was there."

Iris felt her heart clench. "That's...huge."

Jackson rubbed a hand across his face. "Yeah. Part of me hoped to keep some distance from all that, but the thing is, I can't. The Wardens are in my blood. And after everything we've discovered—new mysteries, new dangers—someone has to continue that work."

She stared at the silvery creek. "And that someone is you."

He nodded. "It's my responsibility now. My father drilled that into me for years, and I resisted. But he's right. I can't just walk away. It's bigger than me." He swallowed and turned to face her fully. "Of course, I'll have to resign, but the Wardens are financed by an endowment. I'd be paid."

Not that you need it. Iris couldn't help herself. It seemed odd that he'd even mention the money.

"I need help—a partner."

"But—"

He raised his palm. "Wait. Hear me out."

Iris's heart soared. All the feelings she'd worked to suppress rose to the surface. She loved him. She'd never stopped loving him. But the same conflict arose. She'd be back in that place, following him around as his sidekick. While she knew that he wouldn't let her starve, she'd have no income. No independence.

"Iris, you'd be my partner—with a professional title."

Now Iris was confused. "Are you offering me a job?"

"Well, yes, it's a job. But it's more than that."

"A career?"

"Well, yes, but—" He paused, looking suddenly unsure.

Iris raised an eyebrow. "But...?"

His cheeks flushed with frustration. "I realize saving history and fighting conspiracies are not without a certain amount of danger and stress."

She let out a soft snort of laughter, but it faded when she looked back and saw an expression she'd never seen on his face. It was something like fear.

Jackson took a deep breath, bracing himself against the railing. "I'm trying to give you what you want—a career. I want that for you, too. But I want something more. I want you here with me—at work, at home, everywhere in my life—because I can't imagine a life without you anymore."

She listened in stunned disbelief as tears stung her eyes.

"And yes," he continued, his voice catching, "I realize I'm not great at grand, heartfelt declarations. But there it is." His expression was heartbreakingly earnest. "I love you, and I'm in this for the long haul. If you would...stay."

Iris was paralyzed by the overwhelming but conflicting emotions of joy and fear. Her new job was a big turning point. If she gave it up now, she might never have another chance to build her academic career. And yet, if she took it, she'd be giving up Jackson, a man who'd just opened his heart to her.

While Iris hesitated, Jackson swallowed and reached a trembling hand into his coat pocket. "Iris," he began again, his voice softening, "I'm not just offering you a job or asking you to move in with me." He pulled out a small, worn velvet pouch. "This was my mother's," he admitted shyly. "She wore it until the day she died. My father gave it to me, but I never thought I'd find someone—someone I couldn't imagine living without."

Her eyes went wide.

With a shaky breath, Jackson dropped down to one knee right there at the end of the bridge with the moon overhead. "I'm sorry if I've made this awkward. I know it's sudden. But the truth is, I've been trying to find the right moment. And then you were leaving, and...there's no perfect time anymore, so..." He opened the pouch, revealing a delicate, old-fashioned ring with an oval sapphire surrounded by tiny diamonds.

Iris's hand flew to her mouth. A thousand emotions collided within her, nearly robbing her of speech. The ring caught the moonlight and shimmered.

"Marry me," he whispered. His voice was thick with emotion. "Be my business partner, my friend, my co-adventurer through every crisis and quiet moment. Let's make it work, no matter what."

She stared as tears slipped down her cheeks, and she feared that her heart might burst. A whirlwind of questions spun in her mind while the creek water babbled below. The hush of the winter air seemed to hold them both in suspension. Then her thoughts settled into focus until all that was left was one word.

"Yes."

He looked up with an expression of disbelief. "What?"

Iris laughed. "Yes. Get up before your knees get frostbite." She pulled him up into her arms, kissed him, and held him tightly as though he might slip away.

When they parted, he took her face in his hands. "Are you sure?"

She gazed into his eyes, and time seemed to stand still. All the fear and uncertainty fell away, and she knew this was right.

Jackson didn't wait for an answer. He drew her to

him and kissed her, gently at first, then poured his heart into that kiss.

Thundering hoofbeats echoed over the bridge. Through the shadowy mist, a horse reared, and the Horseman rode on until the last echoes of spectral hoofbeats faded into the trees beyond the Old Dutch Church.

EPILOGUE

Two Weeks Later

Sunlight spilled through the tall windows of Jackson's riverside cottage. The winter snows had receded, and the river flowed quick and cold under a pale blue sky. Boxes—both Iris's and Jackson's, along with some Warden files—lined the hallways.

They sat across a small kitchen table that was strewn with half-open archival containers, each labeled with references to old Warden documents and curiosities. Jackson and Iris each studied leather-bound journals full of cryptic notations.

"Look at this," she said as she tapped a brittle page. "It's a reference to a 'lost timepiece' from 1780, rumored to have some sort of mysterious powers."

Jackson frowned thoughtfully. "If that's real, we'd better find it and make sure it's securely locked away. We already have one volatile artifact to worry about."

She slowly blinked. "Please let there be just the one."

With warmth in his gaze, Jackson reached out to tuck a stray curl behind her ear. Even simple domestic gestures filled her heart. Her cheeks flushed with the quiet knowledge that they were engaged, forging a future as uncertain as any time anomaly but grounded in their resolve to face it together.

Jackson's phone rang from the bedroom charger. He set aside his notes and went to answer it.

Iris continued flipping through the ledger while trying not to grin too widely. Despite the heartbreak and turmoil that brought them here, they had found a place of balance—where they could feed each other's academic curiosity, keep an eye on Sleepy Hollow's lingering mysteries, and build a life as partners in every sense. But most of all, she was happy—simply and thoroughly happy.

Jackson returned, phone still in hand, with his eyebrows raised. "It's Crane. He says there's been an incident in a small town upstate."

"What sort of incident?"

"He didn't say—just some weird goings-on."

Iris arched a brow. "Weird as in...Horseman weird?"

Jackson shrugged, his mouth curving into a wry smile. "Hard to say. He seemed reluctant to discuss it over the phone. He wants us to check it out."

Iris closed the ledger and set it aside, her heart

racing with familiar excitement. "Well, we can't just ignore it, can we?"

He shook his head, clearly torn between exasperation and the thrill of the chase. "No, I guess not. So much for settling into a routine."

Iris grinned, lifting her shoulders in playfulness. "Domestic bliss never stood a chance here, did it?"

Jackson's eyes sparkled with affection. "Apparently not."

As they rose from the table, Iris's mind raced with a mental checklist: grab the field kit, notebook, binoculars, Geiger counter, and other assorted equipment—just in case. She cast a glance at her engagement ring, a subtle reminder that no matter what she faced next, she would have Jackson beside her.

Outside, the sun lit the waters of the Hudson like a broad mirror reflecting the bright sky. As they slipped into their coats and prepared to head out, Jackson lingered for a moment at the door, catching her wrist.

"Hey," he said, his voice low. "You ready for this?"

Iris smiled, letting her free hand rest against his chest. "Aren't I always?"

He pressed a light, warm kiss to her temple. Then, with linked hands and hearts, they stepped onto the porch with the door swinging shut behind them. The hush of the winter morning made their footsteps seem louder. In the distance, seagulls called across the river.

Just before they reached the car, a faint echo of hoofbeats wafted through the still air like a lingering memory. Iris paused and tightened her grip on Jackson's hand. Their gazes locked in unspoken understanding.

They shared a smile, and with one last glance at the winding road, they climbed into Jackson's Rover and set off, wheels crunching over the gravel, leaving Sleepy Hollow to head toward their next adventure.

Behind them, quiet now in the winter sun, the empty cottage hummed with possibility. And somewhere out there, the Headless Horseman still rode—whether mere legend or guardian of time, he was always a reminder that history's shadows ran deep and intertwined with the present. Iris needed no such reminder. She knew he would be there to watch over those who dared to explore the deep currents of history, no matter how far from home or through time they might roam.

THANK YOU!

Thank you for reading! If you enjoyed this book, please consider leaving a review or a rating on Amazon or your favorite bookstore. Your feedback helps other readers discover my work.

BOOK NEWS

Sign up for the J.L. Jarvis Journal for exclusive benefits, including free books, special offers, exclusive content, and updates on new releases: news.jljarvis.com

READING ORDER

Drake & Wilde Mysteries

#1 *Love in the Time of Pumpkins*

#2 *Secrets in the Hollow*

#3 *Shadow of the Horseman*

Standalones

A Kiss in the Rain

App-ily Ever After

Once Upon a Winter

The Red Rose

Highland Vow

Short Stories

Seasons of Love: A Short Story Collection

The Eleventh-Hour Pact

A Christmas Yarn

The Farmer and the Belle

Work-Crush Balance

Cedar Creek

(Can be read in any order)

Christmas at Cedar Creek

Snowstorm at Cedar Creek

Sunlight on Cedar Creek

Pine Harbor

(Reading Order)

#1 *Allison's Pine Harbor Summer*
#2 *Evelyn's Pine Harbor Autumn*
#3 *Lydia's Pine Harbor Christmas*

Holiday House

(Can be read in any order)

The Christmas Cabin
The Winter Lodge
The Lighthouse
The Christmas Castle
The Beach House
The Christmas Tree Inn
The Holiday Hideaway

Highland Passage

(Can be read in any order)

Highland Passage
Knight Errant
Lost Bride

Highland Soldiers

(Reading Order)

#1 *The Enemy*

#2 *The Betrayal*

#3 *The Return*

#4 *The Wanderer*

American Hearts

(Can be read in any order)

Secret Hearts

Forbidden Hearts

Runaway Hearts

For more information, visit jljarvis.com.

Get monthly book news at news.jljarvis.com.

ABOUT THE AUTHOR

J.L. Jarvis is a left-handed former opera singer/teacher/lawyer who writes books. She now lives and writes on a mountaintop in upstate New York.

jljarvis.com

- facebook.com/jljarvis1writer
- x.com/JLJarvis_writer
- instagram.com/jljarvis.writer
- bookbub.com/authors/j-l-jarvis
- pinterest.com/jljarviswriter
- goodreads.com/5106618.J_L_Jarvis
- amazon.com/author/B005G0M2Z0
- youtube.com/UC7kodjlaG-VcSZWhuYUUl_Q

Made in the USA
Las Vegas, NV
03 March 2025